SAVING SARAH

Blissful Bets 2

D1245884

Jennifer Salaiz

POLYAMOUR

Siren Publishing, Inc.
www.SirenPublishing.com

A SIREN PUBLISHING BOOK
IMPRINT: PolyAmour

SAVING SARAH
Copyright © 2010 by Jennifer Salaiz

ISBN-10: 1-61034-000-0
ISBN-13: 978-1-61034-000-7

First Printing: September 2010

Cover design by Jinger Heaston
All cover art and logo copyright © 2010 by Siren Publishing, Inc.

Printed in the U.S.A.

PUBLISHER
Siren Publishing, Inc.
www.SirenPublishing.com

DEDICATION

Good friends are hard to come by. I've been blessed to have some truly amazing people come into my life. Angela, you are one of them. You need to know that no matter what happens I'm here for you. I love you, girlie.

"Imperfection is beauty, madness is genius, and it's better to be absolutely ridiculous than absolutely boring." – Marilyn Monroe

SAVING SARAH

Blissful Bets 2

JENNIFER SALAIZ
Copyright © 2010

Chapter 1

The crowded Cajun restaurant grew louder the moment Sarah spied Evelyn, Julie, Melissa, and their newest friend, Natalie, walk in. For over a year now, the four of them, minus the new brunette, met here for lunch. It was the place where they could relax, be their crazy selves, and also the place where the game Bets came to life. The game itself blossomed into a whole new reason to look forward to the weekends. All thanks to Evelyn.

Out of pure boredom, her genius friend came up with a way to distract themselves until the hot guys came to the island for Spring Break. Now, weeks later, and with the holiday over, Evelyn was officially tied down with two men. She'd conveniently replaced herself in their little game with Natalie, a girl Sarah didn't know.

Even though she had met the brunette on occasion, this technically was their first lunch altogether. The girl's beauty made pretty sound plain, but she couldn't be a day over twenty-five. At thirty-two, Sarah was the oldest out of all the girls. Melissa wasn't that far behind her. For some reason, age had recently started to become a major factor in her everyday thoughts. Even Bets wasn't helping anymore. What would the girls say if they knew she hadn't completed a single one since Evelyn got shacked up?

"I told you Sarah would already be here. How did the sale go, honey?"

Hugging Evelyn, she smiled as they all sat down. "It went smoothly. The clients absolutely adored the house. How was your day? I noticed you weren't in the office for very long."

Her friend's pale face blushed before she quickly looked down. "Yeah, well, I had a trouble leaving the house once I went back to grab my phone."

All the girls started laughing, and Sarah couldn't help but shake her head in humor. "I can't believe they even let you out of the house. Brandon and Stephen pretty much have you locked down as their love slave."

"If I had two men that looked like that, I'd lock myself in," Melissa said, laughing.

"The usual, ladies?"

Sarah turned to see the petite, blonde waitress standing next to her. "Natalie, they pretty much have us memorized here. What would you like to drink?"

"I'll just have what you all are having."

"All right, ladies, I'll have your drinks and food out shortly."

They all watched the waitress leave, and, in sync, they all turned back to Evelyn. "So spill, earlier you said you had some interesting news. I want to know what it is."

A hint of a smile crossed Ev's face. She brushed her black hair back over her shoulder while she leaned forward. "Stephen tells me some of his friends are coming in from out of town. Supposedly, Brandon knows them too, but from what I hear they're *very* unattached. And, from the pictures Stephen showed me, they're jaw-dropping gorgeous. Now, for the fifty million dollar question. Who wants first dibs?"

Every hand at the table rose. "I'm the oldest," Sarah said, smiling, "I get first pick."

"Okay, but don't worry, ladies. From what I've been told, there's a total of five." Evelyn paused while the waitress placed the drinks on the table and walked off.

"So what's the occasion?" Julie asked, picking up her glass.

"Wedding ceremony," Evelyn said, beaming. "You all know my friend Nicole. Well, she's kind of getting married."

"Kind of? To which one, Ayden or Trevor?" Sarah bit her lip trying to figure out her and her friend's ménage relationships. She had no idea how they managed one man, let alone two.

"Both, love. That's why I said kind of. She's marrying both of them, but she's taking Ayden's last name since they met first."

"Weird," Melissa said, grabbing her drink. "No offense, Evelyn. I envy you. I just don't understand the whole threesome thing. Isn't there jealousy with the other partner? Do you have to plan around who and when they get time with you?"

"Not at all. I've never been happier. And I'm ecstatic for Nicole."

The sound of Sarah's phone ringing saved her from the fifty questions running through her mind. Looking at the number marked private on the caller ID, she quickly hit ignore and turned her phone on vibrate. There was only one person she knew that did that, and she wasn't up for dealing with him right now. "Sorry, now where were we?"

"Who was that?" Evelyn said, peering over.

"No one, just a bet that doesn't get the point. You know, I have no idea how he even got my number. How many times do you have to tell a guy no before he gets the picture that you're not interested in going out again?"

"Too many," Melissa said, rolling her eyes.

"Be careful. If you have any problems, call me. I'll have Stephen pay him a visit. I'm sure a police officer showing up at the guy's door will put a stop to it."

"Thanks, Ev. But I'm sure he'll eventually get bored and stop."

The waitress walked up, delivering their food. Sarah immediately got lost in her thoughts. This guy was becoming a pain in her ass. This had gone on for months, and the guy definitely wasn't getting the picture. Tom was one of her first bets, very good looking, but the last thing she needed was a relationship with an arrogant asshole. He carried himself well, could swim in the amount of money he hid in the bank, and completely turned her off with his overpowering personality.

In a daze, she finished off her food, oblivious to her surroundings. It wasn't until Evelyn nudged her that she realized everyone quietly sat, staring at her.

"Sorry, what?"

"We were asking if you were going to the Martini Bar tonight. You know it's Bet Night."

She looked at Melissa and tried to make herself smile. "Of course I am. Have you lost your mind? I wouldn't miss it for the world. I've been looking forward to getting my hands on a good-looking man all week."

Laughing, they all stood and walked outside to their cars. Sarah ran her fingers along the roof of her red Corvette. A lot of people assumed things about her. No one knew the complete and honest truth about who she truly was. The girls thought she wanted some rich man to sweep her off her feet, but that wasn't the case at all. A rich man taking care of her was the last thing she wanted. It was the whole reason why she had her friends target them for bets. Did they really take her for a woman who needed a man to take care of her? No, she'd taken care of herself too long to allow that.

Chapter 2

Sarah stood in the bathroom of her small one bedroom apartment, the same one she'd had for the last ten years. Silence filled the enclosed space, threatening to suffocate her. Her platinum blonde hair hung in waves to her elbows as she took in her reflection. Overall, she looked good. The short, sexy, black dress gave off the impression of what she supposedly would be looking for, but she'd kill to throw on a pair of jeans and a T-shirt.

Out of nowhere, she started shaking. Panic penetrated all the way to her bones. Her mind was screaming for her not to go out tonight. The air even felt electrically charged while she continued to take in her five foot eight inch frame in the mirror. This wasn't the first time this had happened. The last week had been full of panic attacks.

"It's nothing. You're going to be fine, Sarah. You worry too much, that's all. Maybe you need this. What's one guy? After tonight, you can take another break." She looked at herself and laughed. "Great, now you're talking to yourself. It's only downhill from here, darling."

She took one last look in the mirror and grabbed her purse. Tonight, she'd be fine. If she repeated that enough, maybe she would believe it.

Not an hour, and two drinks, later, pop music died out and some song Sarah had never heard before filled the crowded bar. Smoke hung heavily in the air as she weaved her way through the crowds. Music pulsed through her body, courtesy of the increasing volume, but the vibrations from the bass weren't the only things making her crave to be touched.

The blond man dressed in casual jeans and a tight, fitted, black T-shirt was her mark, her bet, and for tonight, her ultimate salvation. He'd numb the needs she'd begun to feel, and his contact would get her through the next few weeks.

Something about the way he stood there staring at her from across the room pulled her in his direction. From the moment he was pointed out to her, she knew she wanted him, had to have him. He'd be the first bet she took in weeks, and she couldn't help but think the wait was well worth it.

"Sarah, wait!"

Quickly, she turned around to spy Julie running toward her. The blonde highlights scattered throughout her dark hair turned neon yellow in the black light. She looked gorgeous in a pair of tight-fitting jeans and a cute, sparkly tank top.

"What? You haven't chosen someone else, have you? I really like this one."

Julie looked toward the blond and smiled. "No, I haven't changed my mind. Just thought I'd come and up the stakes."

"What do you mean?"

Sarah narrowed her eyes. The blue of Julie's eyes blazed mischievously. She let out a giggle, covered her mouth, and then turned to look at the table toward Stephen, Brandon, and Evelyn.

Slowly, Sarah followed her gaze and caught the wink from the pale, dark-haired Brandon. The gold of his eyes nearly made her heart stop. Damn, Evelyn was lucky to have snatched the two hottest guys in Port Aransas area. Despite Brandon's good looks, she didn't miss that mischievous look he had painted across his face. If he had anything to do with Julie's sudden appearance, it wasn't good.

"Brandon said he's got a bet for you. Blondie, *plus,*" Julie smiled even bigger, "him. If you can convince both of them to go home with you, he'll buy your drinks for a year."

Sarah sighed. "Well, for one, Mr. Gorgeous isn't part of our game so he doesn't get to dictate who I decide to go home with. For two, I have no desire to take two men into my bed at this time. One is plenty and complicated enough to get rid of. Two would be impossible. I have no idea how Evelyn even puts up with the both of them. Too much testosterone if you ask me."

She turned to see the new guy in question and froze. Wide chest, taller than any man in the room, he was gorgeous and, heartbreakingly enough, her high school sweetheart. Devon was dressed in cowboy boots, tight jeans, and wore a cowboy hat to cover his dark brown hair. He looked nothing like the carefree rebellious kid she'd dated throughout her teenage years, the one who wore holey jeans and a leather jacket. She felt her chest shake from the rhythm of her heart.

"Hey, are you okay? You look like you've seen a ghost. I think your tan just melted off."

"What?" She looked at Julie, but didn't truly see her. All she could see were memories and images of the two of them. Visions that haunted her every day.

Stop this, Sarah! Just pretend he didn't stomp all over everything you're made of. But she couldn't ignore what happened between them. The fact that she and Devon shared such an intimate past couldn't be overlooked. At seventeen, she'd lost her virginity to him, got pregnant, and then tragically lost the baby when she was only three months along. Too many "what ifs" plagued her every moment, awake or asleep.

"I said are you all right? Geez, what in the hell is the matter with you? You're getting paler by the second. Here, come sit down. If you faint, there's no way in hell I'll be able to lift your tall ass off the floor."

Dizziness escalated the longer she stared at Devon from across the room. Aching in her chest quickly turned to anger. Where exactly had he been? The day after she lost the baby, he disappeared. She'd never heard a word from him. Had everything they shared meant nothing to him? How could someone be so heartless?

Julie led her to the table. Numbly, she sat down across from Evelyn and her men. Without thinking, she picked up her martini and drank it in one shift motion.

"All right, Sarah. Who's the guy?"

"You know Devon?" Brandon asked, leaning toward her.

"She can't know him. He just moved here," Stephen said, looking in the direction of the tall cowboy.

"That's Devon? *The* Devon?" Evelyn reached across the table and grabbed Sarah's hand. "Honey, look at me. Is that him?"

The tears threatened, but she looked up. "Yeah, that's him. Listen, I think maybe I should go. I can't…"

Evelyn squeezed her hand. "Wait, let me explain before you leave upset. He's one of the guys here for the wedding. I'm so sorry. I didn't know. I'll make sure your paths don't cross again. I can't imagine what you're going through."

"What did he do?" Stephen asked.

"Later," Evelyn whispered.

"I have to go. Sarah leaned over toward the wall to grab her purse. She knew she shouldn't have come out tonight. Something kept nagging at her. Why didn't she listen to her intuition? What was she going to do now? Could she avoid him long enough for him to return to wherever he came from? All she knew was that she needed to flee, and fast.

"If he hurt her, I want to know," Stephen said with a low growl from across the table.

Stunned, she looked up. "No, it's not what you think. It wasn't like that at all, not what you're implying, anyway. We went to high school and dated for a while. Let's just say things didn't end well."

"I'm sorry. If I would have known, I never would have said anything," Brandon whispered.

"It's fine, really. Now, I have to go."

Sarah stood up swiftly, only to stand eye level with a very large chest. She didn't even have to guess who it might be. "Fuck," she whispered shakily to herself. She closed her eyes, slowing her breathing. She would *not* show him how scared she felt.

A rough finger brought her chin up so she stared directly into Devon's eyes. The light gray color penetrated into her very soul until she thought she'd surely break into a thousand pieces. Renewed pain fluttered through her chest. He looked so different, yet not. The soft features of boyhood were long gone, transformed into the most gorgeous face she'd ever seen. The thought of what he'd turned into made her heart break even more. She'd missed it all.

Angry at the sensations filling her body, she slapped his hand away from her face. Words wouldn't come, but he didn't have a problem figuring out the unspoken thoughts running through her head. He immediately put his hand down.

"You look more beautiful than I remember. How have you been?"

The hoarseness of his voice somehow invisibly caressed her skin. Her traitorous body leaned in his direction until they weren't more than an inch away from each other.

"I've been great. Never better. You?"

A pained looked passed his features only for a split second, but it was enough to make her stomach flip multiple times. She couldn't ignore how she wasn't the only one affected by their past.

"Fine, I guess."

"Great." Sarah put on a fake smile, trying to find her way around him. "Well, have fun tonight. I was just leaving."

"Don't leave," he whispered. Softly, his hand wrapped around her arm, immobilizing her. Heat rushed to her very core. Trembling immediately took over her body. The panicky feeling rushed back through her until she couldn't breathe.

The sound of glass breaking caused everyone to spin around. Melissa stood there, staring at them angrily. Sarah wasn't sure whether to laugh or cry. Melissa, being closer to her age, was the only one who personally knew Devon and their situation. And the girl was a force to be reckoned with when she was pissed.

"You son of a bitch." She stalked forward, her red hair flying out behind her. "Get the hell away from my friend. Don't you think you've hurt her enough? Do you have any idea what she went through when you just disappeared?"

Her friend barely came to his upper stomach. With her hands, she pushed him back, and embraced Sarah.

"Stay the hell away from her, or…or, I'll kick your ass myself."

Brandon stood up, but Devon put up his hand for him to sit down. "You were always a feisty little thing, Melissa. I'm sorry about what happened with Sarah, but I didn't come back to cause trouble. It seems I've accumulated some responsibilities in this area, and I've decided since I'm already here for the wedding, I might as well move back."

Melissa's face turned almost as red as her hair. She started to advance toward him when Sarah quickly grabbed her arm. "Moving back? Are you serious? Fucking great. You know, you had responsibilities before you left, asshole."

"Melissa, that's enough," Sarah whispered. "I'm fine, really. I was just leaving. It seems I have a date with a very good-looking blond."

Confused, she turned in the direction of where Sarah pointed her finger. The anger left her face as a smile began to form. Her friend raised an eyebrow at Devon appearing to say, *look what you lost out on.* "Ah, I see. Well, you have fun tonight. Be careful and call me when you get home."

Sarah took one last look at the man who broke her heart and walked over to her original bet. She needed this more than ever. The last person she wanted to think about was Devon. If she went home alone, she'd be up all night trying to figure out the reasons for his desertion. It was pointless. Instead, she'd block him out the only way she knew how, by Bets.

Approaching, she ate up the man's powerful appearance. Damn, he was something else. Even with his clothes on, she could see how built his body was. Vision of running her tongue over every inch of his hard muscles made her insides tighten. She took a deep breath and extended her hand. "Hi, I'm Sarah."

The blond beamed an impressive smile at her. He had full lips, a square chin, and the greenest eyes she'd ever seen. "I'm Gavin, nice to meet you," he said, bringing her fingers to his lips. Her body instantly came alive. The surprise at how powerful his effect was had her nipples tingling and her pussy all too wet. "I saw you earlier and thought you were coming over here, but you left."

"My friend needed to ask me something. It was no big deal. So, I'm not usually so rushed, but I really want to get out of here. I thought maybe I would ask you a question."

He cocked his head to the side, staring intently into her face. She couldn't help but bite her bottom lip as heat coursed through her body. His sweet-smelling breath brushed her face as he leaned in closer. "Shoot. What would you like to know?"

Whatever Sarah was going to ask vanished the moment she looked into his gaze. With every second the slipped by, the green color seemed to intensify, captivating her. "Wow, you have beautiful eyes." The connection she felt toward him jolted through her body. Something about this man fascinated her and eased the pain from Devon. Yes, Gavin was definitely what she needed. He'd fuck her ex from her head, and she had no plans of calling it a night until he did.

"Thank you, so do you." His hand hesitated just above her cheek. She leaned into his touch, momentarily lost to everything but him. His voice drew her from the fantasies playing out in her mind. "So, you wanted to ask me something?"

"Umm, my question, right. Well, I'm leaving, and I thought I'd see if you wanted to join me."

His hand fell away as a confused expression crossed his face. "Just like that? You mean I don't have to take you to an early breakfast and try to seduce you? You just want me to leave with you, no questions asked?"

"That's exactly what I'm saying."

Sarah internally groaned, knowing how ridiculous it sounded. Usually, she tried to make it more inconspicuous. Devon was really screwing up her head. The need to flee overpowered everything, and she hated not being in control.

"Well, it's forward, but sure. I'd love to leave with you."

She sighed in relief. She really didn't feel like walking out of the bar by herself. Especially, since she already made it sound like her date knew about their departure. It wouldn't have looked very good if it was completely obvious that she'd lied.

Taking a peak at the table, she noticed Stephen and Devon arguing. About what, she wasn't sure, but she wasn't sticking around to find out. She grabbed Gavin's hand and began to weave through the crowd.

The moment her eyes connected with Devon's, she tripped over her own feet. He was livid. She'd never seen him so angry in all of her life. Gavin righted her before she completely fell on her face, but she hardly noticed. All she could see was the way the once love of her life was affected by her being with someone else.

"Are you all right?"

Sarah looked up startled. "Yeah, I'm fine. Let's get out of here. Your car or mine?"

"Mine, if that's all right."

"Sounds great."

They walked out into the humid air, and she was quickly pulled to the far end of the parking lot. Gavin stopped in front of a red Corvette, and she laughed.

"What's so funny?"

She turned to the right and pointed three cars down. "That's mine."

"Glad to see you have excellent taste," he said, winking.

He stood not inches away from her. Taking a deep breath to still her racing heart, she stepped closer to him, pushing her body against his. "Where do you want to go?"

"Tell me what you need. Are you rushed, or do we have time?"

A shiver raced over her body at how deep his voice lowered. The huskiness left her reaching for him. Tightly, she held his shirt in her fists, trying to fight the way he oddly affected her. There was no pretending with him. She didn't have to. Her body seemed to have a life of its own when she got close.

"I have all night. There's no rush."

"Then I know just where to go. I saw it as I came into town. You're okay with going to a hotel room, right?"

"Yes." The word left her mouth in a whisper. She couldn't wait to see what he could give her. Oh yes, she needed this. Sarah almost couldn't believe her luck. Finally, she would feel again. Numbness had been her friend for far too long. Tonight, she'd submit and experience the pleasure women longed to feel, and she'd feel it with Gavin.

Chapter 3

Soft, full lips caressed hers gently. Parting hers, just a fraction, she felt his warm tongue trace the tip of hers. Delicious shivers shot down her body. Opening her mouth farther, she drank in his taste, letting the flavor take over her senses. He tasted of beer and something sweeter, something so intoxicating she pulled his body closer into hers, wrapping her arms around his neck. The feeling of her breasts against the hardness of his chest caused her to moan.

"Sarah, let's get the hell out of her before I fuck you right here in this parking lot."

Dazed, she pulled back and nodded, getting in the car. Gavin shut the door behind her, and she watched him run around to get it in. It didn't take him long to pull out of the parking lot and head to the first nice hotel they came across. Quietly, she waited in the car while he checked in.

The sound of her phone caught her off guard. She pulled it out of her purse and stared. The number was marked private. Well shit.

"Hello? Hello?"

Silence. She hung up and turned it off. She knew who it was, but it didn't matter *who* would have called. Nothing was going to stop her tonight. Bets never affected her like this, and she wasn't about to get distracted by anyone who might think to bother her.

Gavin came back to the car and got in, parking toward the back of the building. He sat there silently for a few moments and then turned toward her. "You sure you want to do this? We can stop now if you've changed your mind."

Sarah leaned across the seat and pressed her lips against his. "Let's go inside, shall we?" The need to continue kissing almost made it impossible for her to sit back against the seat. The intensity with which she wanted him definitely couldn't be ignored.

"Yes, let's go."

They quickly got out and walked to the door directly in front of them. Sarah molded her body to his. She almost felt the sparks flying from their chemistry.

The sound of the door closing hardly registered. All she could feel were his hands trailing up the back of her thighs, pushing her dress up. Tightly, she gripped around his neck, pulling his hard cock into her stomach. A moan poured into her mouth at the pressure. From the sounds he made and the heavy rhythm of his breathing, she felt sure he wanted her just as much as she wanted him.

Cool air brushed against the bottom of her ass as her dress lifted higher. She trembled while his fingers slid up, gripping the inside of her upper thighs. He was so close to touching her pussy, she shook from the anticipation.

"God, you taste so good."

He began kissing her again, lifting her to sit at his waist. She could feel them moving toward the bed, and when he lowered her, the comforter cooled her heated skin. The only thing she could focus on was the thick bulge that rested at her most private place. The power with which she wanted this stranger somewhat scared her. This wasn't who she was. Sarah was known amongst her friends for being cold to men at times, but with Gavin, she was different. For the first time since Devon left, she was tempted to keep this stranger, keep him forever.

His weight lifted off of her, and she opened her eyes. She instantly connected with his gaze. They never broke contact while he took off her clothes. The muscles in his chest flexed as he pulled the shirt over his head. She stared, fascinated. He began unbuttoning his pants, and she turned her attention to the ceiling. The last thing she wanted to do was make him feel uncomfortable from her ogling. It didn't help that the possessive feelings for him continued to grow with every mounting second.

"I've never done this before, seriously." Gavin's whisper died as her nipple was sucked into his mouth. The pure shock of the pleasant sensations caused her to cry out.

Sarah's voice echoed through the room while she weaved her fingers in his hair. She wished she could say she'd never done this before, but she couldn't lie. These encounters were what she used to live for, how she eluded the pain when it became too much.

Teeth pulled at her tight nub until she thought she would die from the pleasure. His large arm wrapped under her waist, and she felt the brush of his fingers trailing along her smooth folds. In small circles, he messaged the wetness into her skin.

Increasing the pressure of her hands, she gripped his shoulders. Gavin hadn't even entered her yet, and she was so close to coming. Sarah couldn't wait to feel his cock slide into her, to somehow make this connection she felt stronger.

"Gavin, please."

"Say my name again," he whispered huskily.

"Gavin," Sarah moaned.

One finger entered her pussy slowly, reaching deep inside. She could feel her nails sinking into his smooth skin. The arm behind her back pulled down, making her back arch farther. With the new angle, his finger caressed just the right spot to make her body burst into spasms.

The warmth of his tongue brushed her opening, running along the finger he still had inside of her. It was enough to prolong her orgasm until she was screaming from the bliss. After she felt sure it finally ended, he continued to trace her pussy with his tongue. Heat repeatedly coursed through her body.

"I could do this forever. Fuck, you taste even better, here. This pussy was meant to be cherished." He sucked her into his mouth and let out a small growl as he pulled back. "Sarah, you wouldn't happen to have protection, would you?"

She blinked, trying to bring the room back into focus. "My purse." The sound of her voice was almost unrecognizable. Gavin shifted on the bed, and he handed her the black clutch. She opened it, fumbling with the contents until her hand connected with the package.

The sound of the wrapper tearing made delicious currents travel down her body. His weight settled over her, and she looked into his gaze as he slowly began to enter her. She could feel her eyes widening at his thickness, but trying to keep them open became a chore. The width of his cock was something she hadn't felt in a long time. He seemed to fill every inch of the inside of her body.

"Open your eyes, honey. I want you to look at me while I fuck that sweet, little pussy of yours."

She obeyed without thought. Muscles in his arms flexed as he lifted to deepen his thrusts.

"I was serious about never doing this before. I'm just not that type of guy."

Of course he wasn't. If he hadn't said anything, she sure as hell wouldn't have pegged him for the one night stand type. "I believe it." She continued to take in the muscles in his chest, but was amazed at how her eyes always came back to his.

"You belong to me. I know how odd and crazy this probably sounds to you, but it's the truth." He lowered, and the words were whispered in her ear. "Can you feel our chemistry, Sarah?"

Rapid thoughts rushed through her head. "I don't know what I feel. A part of me is strangely…attracted to you, and not just looks. This feels right."

He took a deep breath while his cock pushed deeper. "But this, what we're doing, you will see me afterward, right?"

Here was the million dollar question. Her unstable spark flickered. It was possessive and controlling. She wanted to say he wasn't going anywhere, ever again. Then reality hit. What was happening? He talked as if they were connected, and she knew this wasn't her usual behavior. The strange sensations circling her heart screamed to say yes to his question. Even her mind felt as though it were trying to convince her that this guy was meant to be in some part of her life. Nervously, her stomach twisted, only intensifying the pleasure.

Could she see him again? Devon immediately rushed into her mind. If he was moving back that only meant one thing—she'd be plagued by his appearances at random places. Could she open herself up to start something that could possibly be the beginnings of a relationship? What about Bets, the girls? Evelyn still was a part of their group even though she didn't bet anymore. Could she do the same?

"Sarah, answer me. Can we see each other after this?"

She didn't think. She went with her gut instinct. "Yes. God, yes. Come here."

Pulling his upper body against her breasts, she felt him surge to unbelievable depths inside of her pussy. They both moaned, tightening their arms around each other. Every possible inch inside of her got caressed and pleasured at the same time. The muscles flexed in his arms while he lifted one side of his body away from her. She couldn't help but stare in awe.

* * * *

Gavin watched the most beautiful woman he'd ever met moan beneath him. He was only supposed to be here long enough for the wedding, but he couldn't leave now. Not with Sarah being meant for him. Their link was instantaneous and undeniable.

Would she go back to Houston with him? He didn't think so. There was an aura about her that said she liked to be in control. It wasn't the colors surrounding her body that he could see, but more the feeling he got from the invisible shield. And, boy, was he going to have his hands full.

One thing he knew for sure, and that was that she'd been hurt, and badly. It didn't matter. He was determined to heal her, however he could. He knew he couldn't rush things. It would only push her away, but damn, he couldn't imagine being away from her for a single moment.

Tightening of her pussy gripped painfully around his cock as her orgasm beckoned. His lips lowered to hers as he continued to thrust. The need to mark her as his overpowered him. But he couldn't, not yet. If she chose not to be with him, it would torture her. Even now, she'd always feel the pain, but not like she would if they were truly bonded. He couldn't put the lovely blonde through that, no matter how much pain it brought him.

Sweetness brushed against his tongue as they kissed. He could feel her breathing become labored as she fought against her release. She was so close. He could tell by how she clutched him. With a swift motion, he plunged inside of her, causing her to scream while tremors wracked her body. Unfortunately, it was his undoing. Ecstasy rushed through him as the cum poured from his cock.

Chapter 4

Sarah stood outside of her car while she waved goodbye to Gavin. The sun was just coming up over the city of Corpus Christi. Her Corvette was only one of three cars still in the parking lot of the Martini Bar. She smiled as she watched her car's twin drive off. After giving her phone number and address to this guy, she felt lighter, happier, than she had in years.

"This could work," she said, opening her door. "A new beginning." She threw her purse into the passenger side seat and screamed as hands gripped her hips, pulling her back.

"No, it won't work." Devon turned her around to face him. His gray eyes were bloodshot, and he looked tired but still just as angry as when she last saw him.

"What in the hell do you think you're doing? Were you waiting here all night?"

"We need to talk."

Sarah pulled her arm out of his grasp. "I think the time for talking is long over. What could we possibly need to discuss now?"

"Why I left."

Tears began to cloud her vision, but she refused to let them fall. "I think you just summed it up perfectly. You left. You didn't want to be with me. Your actions proved that."

"You're wrong. I've always loved you, Sarah. Nothing's changed that, and nothing ever will."

"I don't want to hear this. Why are you doing this to me?"

She scrambled backward. The proximity at which she stood caused the ache in her chest to intensify. How many times had they held each other while he whispered lies of unconditional love? It may have been years ago, but the memories never faded, nor the pain.

"I'm trying to right a wrong. I love you. I had to leave. Not because I wanted to, but because I had no other choice. If I would have taken you with me, you'd have hated me forever."

"Quit talking in riddles and tell me what the hell was so important that you left me the day after I lost our baby!"

The tears betrayed her and poured down her cheeks. The look of pain on his face only made more fall. She felt torn. A part of her wanted him to comfort her. For him to tell her some outrageous story so she could understand and get over this pain, but she knew what he did was unforgivable. The anger made her want to hurt him as much as he hurt her.

"My father. Well, he died, leaving his responsibilities to me. Those obligations forced me move to Waco. I didn't want it, but I had to go."

"What responsibilities or obligations were more important than being with me to mourn our loss?"

The sound of tires screeching in the parking lot caused both of them to turn toward the red Corvette that came flying in. The look Gavin had on his face as he slammed his door and approached held none of the passion she saw earlier. The quickness with which his large frame moved toward them left her stunned.

"What in the hell is going on here?" He quickly pulled Sarah next to his body, protecting her with his arm.

Devon narrowed his eyes, taking a step toward them. He looked menacing, ready to attack her new lover, but Gavin didn't budge an inch. "I don't think that's any of your damn business. How about you get back in that death trap of yours and leave."

"No, I'm not going anywhere, ever," Gavin snapped.

Sarah could feel the tension thick in the air. She wasn't sure what to do or who to side with. As much as she wanted to know what

Devon was talking about, she sure as hell didn't want to be alone with him.

"Gavin, what are you doing here?"

"I wanted to make sure you left safely. I'm glad I came back. Do you want me to follow you home?"

Sarah looked toward Devon. "Yes, we were done here."

"No, we weren't. I need to explain."

"Later. Now's not that time, Devon. I'm tired, and I want to go home."

Her ex turned toward the tall blond holding her and glared in his direction. The saying, "if looks could kill," crossed her mind, but she quickly broke their stare at each other.

"Gavin, let's go. Devon, I'll call your mother later. You are staying there, correct?"

"No, I got an apartment until my house is built. But you can call her. She'd love to hear from you. She asks about you all the time."

"Does she have your number?"

"Yes, she'll give it to you."

"All right. I'll talk to you later."

She watched Devon hesitantly walk off and get into an oddly familiar looking truck. Gavin remained silent until he was gone. "Do you still want me to follow you home?"

"No, I think I'll be okay now. Thank you for coming to check on me."

"It was no problem. I take it you two share a past?"

Sarah could have laughed at that statement. *Did we ever.* As much as she wanted to lie and brush off what her new lover had just seen, she couldn't lie to him. If she was going to continue to see him, and she had every intention of doing so then she needed to tell the truth. "Yeah, you could say that."

Gavin pressed his lips against her forehead. "I'm sorry he caused you pain. I'm only a call away if you need anything. I'll come as quickly as I can."

"I do…need something," Sarah whispered, looking up to meet his eyes.

"Anything, just ask."

"Dinner?" *With you as dessert.*

He laughed, and for some unexplainable reason, her heart felt it. "What time, gorgeous?"

"Early. Six?"

"Six, it is. I'll see you then."

Sarah watched as he got in his car and waited for her to leave. She pulled out of the parking lot and headed toward the island while he turned and went into the opposite direction. Throbbing erupted in her head while she fought to keep her eyes on the road. Soon, she'd be home, and she could get some much needed rest before dinner tonight. Just the thought of going on an actual date made her heart thump harder. Oh, how she prayed she was doing the right thing.

Chapter 5

The sound of the phone ringing echoed in the back of Sarah's mind. Sleepily, she reached for it, clicking it open without looking at whose number was on the outside. "Hello?"

Silence filled the line. "Hello?" Still nothing. "Look, this is getting old. Who in the hell is this? Tom, this is you, isn't it?"

"Quite a show you put on earlier. Who's the cowboy? He seemed to melt the ice that surrounds your heart. I've never seen you cry before."

"That's none of your damn business. If you call me again, I'm calling the cops."

The line disconnected, and Sarah looked toward her clock. She had to blink twice to make sure she read the time right. "Five fifty!" With her adrenaline pumping, her legs almost gave out the moment her feet hit the ground.

How in the hell did she sleep so long? Sarah jumped in the shower and washed as quickly as she could. Her hair took the longest, but in record time, she was running to her closet to find some clothes. A knock on her door caused her to groan.

"First date in years and I fuck it up."

Throwing on her robe, she walked to the door. Slowly, she opened it only a few inches. Her jaw dropped when she noticed it wasn't Gavin, but Devon standing there.

"How did you know where I lived?"

His smile made her stomach tighten. "I noticed your car. I live three doors down," he said pointing. "Since the parking spaces are marked it wasn't hard for me to figure out which one you lived in."

"Well, I'm getting ready for a date. I know we need to finish our talk, but right now really isn't the time." The shaking of her body increased the longer he stood staring at her.

The smile faded from his face and an unexplainable feeling stabbed her heart. "Sarah, I know I don't deserve to be forgiven for what I've done, but if you'll just hear me out, I'll leave. If you don't want to see me again after that, then, it's up to you."

"Couldn't we do this later? Really, I'm running extremely late. Gavin will be here any moment."

Devon pushed his way inside at the mention of Gavin's name. "You act like I haven't seen you naked before. I'll tell you as you get dressed."

"You are not seeing me naked! You are not allowed to leave this living room. Talk loud."

Sarah ran to her room, not wasting any time. She quickly pulled on her white lace panties and bra. Looking around the room for her hair clip, she noticed Devon wasn't talking. Her eyes landed on the dresser mirror, and she could see him watching her from the living room. She froze.

"I didn't see anything other than what you're wearing now. I promise."

She stalked to the living room until she faced him. "You want me to believe that? You were watching me get dressed."

"Sarah," he whispered huskily.

Immediately, a pull made her lean closer. "Devon, I think you should leave." She could barely talk, let alone fight what her mind kept telling her to do. The urge to touch him made her pussy ache. Flashes of them together all those years ago refreshed in her mind. Fuck, he was an amazing lover, even back then when they were so young.

Fingertips trailed along her bra strap down to the swell of her breast. "You don't know how many times I dreamed of you, just like this. The smell of your skin still haunts me."

Sarah was pulled gently into his arms. The heat coming from his body was so inviting, she wanted to snuggle in closer. Just like him, everything about them together plagued her life.

"Kiss me, Sarah. Please, let me taste you."

She jerked back so suddenly she fell on her ass. "Get out, right now. I don't know what your intentions are for coming here, or doing what you just did, but I don't have time for this shit. Date, remember?"

He smiled and tipped his cowboy hat. "No, I don't think I could forget the fact that my future wife is about to date one of my rivals, but go ahead. I hope you have fun."

"Future wife! You have lost your mind. Get out!"

Sarah tried to hide the shock caused by his statement, but she couldn't. She literally pushed him out of the door. Gavin stood there waiting with grocery bags in one hand.

"I heard yelling. Are you all right?"

She looked toward Devon and stepped back into her apartment. "I'm fine. As you can tell, I'm not dressed. I woke up late. Why don't you come in while I get some clothes on?" She turned to Devon. "You can explain things *later*. I'll call you. Do not come by again without me knowing."

He laughed and turned to Gavin. "Houston, is it? I was Waco, but not anymore. Watch yourself. If you so much as brush your teeth against her skin, I'll be there to tear you apart."

Sarah looked back and forth between them, completely puzzled. The rage coming from both men only increased her own anger. "What in the hell are you talking about, Devon?"

Gavin's body relaxed. He smiled and ran his free palm along her cheek. "I'll let Sarah choose before I go that far. But, for your information, I've already cleared things with Marcos, and Ayden said he'd be glad to have me. So, it looks like I'm a permanent resident of this little island town, too."

Devon growled, making Sarah jump. "Someone better explain things to me because I have no idea what in the hell you both are talking about. And what's Ayden have to do with this? Are you *both* here for the wedding?"

"Yes," Gavin said quietly. "But I'm not going back afterward. I'm staying."

Before she could say anything one of the neighbors walked by, gawking at her appearance. Sarah could feel her cheeks burn from embarrassment. "I'm getting dressed, dammit. Gavin, come inside. Devon, we'll talk later."

Without even waiting, Sarah turned around and walked quickly to her room. She threw on the first pair of jeans she could find and grabbed a red and black flannel shirt. It wasn't anywhere near flattering, but from the looks of things, Gavin planned to cook. She might as well show him how she looked when she wasn't out. That's what dating was all about, wasn't it? It was two people trying to impress the other, while all the time pretending to be what the other person likes. Not her, not this time. She'd be herself, and it was take it or leave it.

"Sorry about you walking up on that," she said, coming into the kitchen. "I thought he was you. If it wouldn't have been for the phone ringing, I'd probably still be asleep."

He smiled, removing the contents from the bag. "Well, then, who do I have to thank for waking Sleeping Beauty?"

Sarah immediately tensed. He stopped and stepped closer to her. "This person makes you feel uncomfortable? Who was it?"

"How do you know he makes me uncomfortable?"

Gavin cupped her cheeks, staring deeply into her eyes. "I can feel how stressed this person makes you feel. I know it sounds weird. Call me sensitive, or whatever, but I don't want to have to hide it from you. I can feel other people's emotions. At least, for the last few years, anyway."

She felt a little shocked but knew he was telling the truth. As odd as it seemed to her, she believed him. "His name is Tom. I met him a while back. He's become a pest, so to speak."

"No, it's more than that." He studied her face. "Have you called the police?"

Sarah laughed it off, pulling back from his reach. "No, of course not. He'll get the picture."

Gavin took a step closer filling in the distance she put between them. "Don't always trust everyone you meet. There are some bad people out there. Not everyone *gets the picture*, as you like to put it. Just be careful. If you want me to tell him to stop, I will."

She nodded and watched him walk back to the food. For the first time, she felt scared of Tom. Before it was just an annoyance, but Gavin's warnings had somehow sunk in. She recalled his words earlier on the phone.

"Gavin…never mind."

"No, tell me. You wanted to say something. Do you want me to talk to him?"

"Maybe you should if he calls again. He said something that I didn't really catch until now."

He looked over at her curiously. "Like what?"

"He said he saw what happened this morning between the three of us. I really think he was watching."

Gavin's hand froze on the package of pasta. "He's watching you?" She didn't miss anger that flared across his features. "Is this the first time he's mentioned doing something like this?"

Closing her eyes, Sarah thought over everything he ever said, which wasn't much. "Yes, I believe so. Mainly, there's just silence, but this morning I actually addressed him. He answered back. When I threatened to call the police, he hung up on me."

"Well, maybe you scared him, but I do want the phone next time there's a number you don't recognize."

She nodded and walked over, handing him a pot. Quietly, they stood side by side while they put the spaghetti to boil and the sauce to cook. It felt strange for her to be doing this with anyone. Especially, someone she just met. But something about Gavin made her feel at ease. She instantly had trusted him. A part of her wanted to say fuck the food, and just go to the bedroom, but something stopped her from doing so.

"I don't think us watching the water is going to make it boil any faster," he said laughing

She turned toward him and smiled. "I think you may be right. Sorry, I'm just not used to this. I'm not sure what to do."

He pulled her into his arms. "You don't have to do anything. Did I mention how beautiful you look, by the way? I like you dressed like this. I'm glad I decided we should stay in instead of going out somewhere. Sarah, there's something I need to tell you about myself, and I'm not really sure how you're going to take it."

Questions filled her mind, but she wasn't sure what he needed to confess. They had just met each other.

"What is it?"

Gently, he pulled her to sit down at the table. She watched him trace the wood with his fingertip while he shifted in the chair. "Sarah, when I say this, you have to trust me, okay?"

"All right," she said uneasily.

"I got into town last night and drove straight to the bar. I don't know why, but I had this need to go there. I've never even heard of that place, but when I saw you, I knew you were the reason. With my kind, it's like that. We show up or go places for reasons unknown to us. Everything revolves around the pull."

"Your kind? You mean intuitives, people who are sensitive like you?"

She watched him open his mouth and then close it. "I don't want to lie to you. No, not sensitives. I am one of those, but that's not what I meant. I think this conversation isn't ready to happen yet. Let's just forget the last part. Just know that my intentions are genuine. I plan on sticking around. That's what I meant to say. Plus, you should know I have a daughter. She lives with her mother, but I do get her on occasion."

Her mouth dropped open in surprise. "Really? Thank you for telling me. What's her name?"

"Annabelle. She's five." He pulled out a picture from his wallet and handed it to her. Blonde ringlets surrounded her beautiful face. Sarah couldn't help but smile. If she would have had a daughter, would she look like this? Would she have her blonde hair or Devon's dark hair? She handed the picture back to him.

"She's beautiful."

He smiled. "Thank you, yes, yes she is. And, completely spoiled, thanks to me."

They both laughed together until Gavin turned serious. "I do plan to live in this town, Sarah. How do you feel about that?"

She smiled, but still couldn't shake weird vibe she received from the riddles he spoke of earlier. "I want you to stick around. I feel something, this trust or closeness to you that I can't explain. It's weird. I've never felt this connected to anyone besides..." Her smile disappeared.

"That guy, Devon, was it?"

"Yes, Devon. He used to make me feel this way."

Gavin stared at her awhile and grabbed her hand. "Does he still? I mean, you two obviously share something to have such emotions toward each other, but do you feel a pull toward him? All I get from you when you're together is pain and confusion."

"Gavin..." Sarah took a deep breath, trying not to get too expressive. "Devon and I were together all through high school. At the end of our senior year, I got pregnant." Shit, she really hadn't wanted to get into this conversation yet, but if she wanted to keep him, she needed to be truthful, even if it was a lot sooner than she would have liked. "When I was three months along, I lost the baby.

For reasons he still hasn't explained, he left me the next day." She took a ragged breath. "I loved him with everything I had, and he broke my heart. So, now that you know, you can understand how I'm not sure how I feel about him anymore."

"I see."

He was so quiet she wasn't sure what he could possibly be thinking. She wouldn't blame him for running out and never looking back. Not very many men would want to mix themselves up with the drama that was establishing itself in her life. Of course, not many people would even be having this conversation on the first freaking date.

"If you want to leave, I understand."

He looked up so quickly she had to blink twice to see if she'd seen correctly. "Sarah, I'm not going anywhere. I'm sorry you thought the worst. I was just thinking about what I should do about Devon. He seems just as determined to be in your life as I am. You have to see that."

"No, he just wants to clear his conscience. After that, I'll probably never hear from him again."

Rich laughter made her jump. "Don't be so sure of that. He's alph…he's used to being in control. He won't back down easily."

Sarah stood and walked to the stove. She didn't agree with Gavin, but she didn't feel like arguing. She stirred the sauce while her mind played over the events of the last twenty-four hours. Damn, what had she got herself into?

Chapter 6

Dinner was delightful while Sarah and Gavin shared random stories, but everything felt off. They cleaned up the kitchen as Sarah went through her thoughts. Too many memories she wanted to share had Devon in them, and she sure as hell didn't want to mention her adventures during Bets. It felt weird having to pause to think about something else to say.

Arms wrapped around her waist, pulling her body into Gavin's. His breath against her neck caused heat to pulse through her body. Slowly, she turned around in his arms to look at him.

"Did you enjoy dinner?" His forehead rested against hers as he closed his eyes and inhaled deeply. She noticed he seemed to do that a lot.

"Yes. I had a great time."

Soft lips pressed into hers, and his taste exploded inside her mouth. Before she knew it, she was clutching to him, breathless. The hardness of his cock pressed into her stomach. She loved that feeling. Knowing how much he wanted her gave her the control she loved.

"I think I should go. I don't want you to think this is why I opted for us to stay here."

For reasons Sarah couldn't fathom, she gripped to him tightly. "Don't leave. Stay the night with me. I don't think this is the only reason you're here. I just…" She trailed off, shocked by the way she was acting. This wasn't like her. Where was the independent woman who didn't need a man?

"I'm sorry. I don't know what came over me. If you want to leave, I understand." She stepped back. A feeling of being physically torn caused her heart to ache, just like with Devon. A part of her didn't want him to leave, ever. It was too much, too soon.

"It's not that I want to leave. I just think, for now, it'll be better. If you want, we can do this tomorrow. That is, if you don't have other plans."

She looked up. "No, no plans. Same time?"

"Sounds great." He kissed her lips softly and then walked to the door. She was half tempted to drag his ass back and lock them both in.

The moment he was gone, Sarah collapsed on the couch. What in the hell was wrong with her? Maybe she was losing it. Sarah clicked on the TV and settled for the preview channel. It wasn't long before she grew bored and turned it off. Both Devon and Gavin kept popping into her head, and she wasn't sure what to do about it. Should she call her ex and get that part of her life over with so she could move on with the new part?

As much as she didn't want to, she knew what had to be done. It wasn't a conversation that could happen over the phone. She'd have to find him and confront this problem face to face.

Sarah stood and walked outside. The truck he drove was parked three spaces down from hers. She walked along the sidewalk until it turned, and she stood in front of his door. He opened it before she knocked.

"I was hoping you'd come by."

"Let's get this over with." Sarah walked around him into his apartment. She stumbled to a stop, looking around. Pictures of them, together, covered almost every available space on the walls. The breath completely left her body at the memories so clearly in front of her.

"Sarah, why don't you have a seat? You know, I've had these pictures with me the whole time I've been gone. Even if I couldn't be with you, having the memories displayed helped."

Numbly, she sat down on his blue cushions. "Why did you leave me? Go ahead and finish." She tried to control her emotions but knew it wouldn't be long before she broke. Just seeing their past surrounding her caused an ache like nothing she'd ever experienced. The need to flee kept pushing against her brain. A picture caught her attention, and she immediately stood, walking over to look at it.

The girl looked so young. She and Devon were kissing on the beach. The pink and orange of the sky, as the sun set, looked faded with time. But she remembered that day as clearly as if it had just been taken. It was shortly after she found out she was pregnant. They were so much in love then. At least she thought they were.

"That one is my favorite. We were so happy then. Do you remember?"

"Every day, Devon." She sighed. "Now go on."

"Sarah." He turned her around to look at him. "What I'm about to say cannot leave this room. You have to promise me that when I tell you, you're not going to freak out. It's going to sound outrageous and unbelievable, but I promise you that what I'm saying is the truth."

"Just tell me, Devon. I don't care what it is. I need to know."

"Do you remember the summer I went through all those problems? I got in a lot of trouble with my mother for the stupid, reckless things I did."

"Yes, of course, but what does that have to do with anything?"

Devon pulled her to the couch so they could both sit down. "That summer, I found out something that changed my life. My father visited for the first time and told me something so unbelievable, he had to end up showing me for himself. I have a feeling that's exactly what I'm going to have to do with you."

"Devon, just tell me," Sarah said, losing patience.

"I know everyone's heard legends about werewolves."

Sarah's palm connected with his cheek before she knew she'd raised it. "You are not fucking going there, Devon. I think I deserve a better excuse than that."

"Just here me out, please. It's the reason why I had to leave. When my father died, they expected me to take over. I haven't found a replacement good enough for me to come back, until now."

Sarah's palm connected with his cheek, again, but she didn't stop at that. She went wild swinging her fists, and attacking him. "What kind of piss poor excuse is that? You expect me to believe that crap, Devon! A freaking legacy you took over from your father? You son of bitch!"

Sarah jumped up and headed for the door. A fucking werewolf. Ridiculous! Next he'd be telling her that little green men ate breakfast with him every Sunday, and fairies really did exist.

Devon leaped from the couch so fast, he beat her to the door before she got two steps away from where'd she had been sitting.

"I knew you wouldn't believe me. Don't make me show you. I don't want to scare you, but I need you to believe and trust me."

"Either you grow fur or else I'm screaming bloody murder until you move your ass out of my way. Fucking werewolf. You must think I'm the most gullible person in the..."

Horrified, she watched Devon's features morph. The trembling of his body was quickly followed by his limbs contorting. Clothes fell to the floor and suddenly she was staring at a very large, black wolf. She couldn't move, couldn't speak. It was like she'd just seen a horrible car accident. It was impossible, and yet she couldn't deny what was standing in front of her. Tears streamed down her face as her reality crashed to the ground. It couldn't be real.

Stumbling backward, she fell over her feet and landed hard on the floor. She continued to crawl backwards until her back pressed against the wall and there was nowhere else to go. No words would come for a long time.

He hadn't so much as moved since he'd changed. She was almost afraid to speak, but there were so many questions and she didn't even know where to begin. Sucking in a deep breath, she forced the words out "You really are a wolf, aren't you? I thought..."

He turned human just as fast. The powerful, nude body that stood before her was not the same one she'd seen when he left. "You had to know. I didn't have a choice. Sarah, I couldn't take you with me. It's dangerous at times, and I knew you would be safer here. If I kept contact with you, a rival could have found out. But you *had* to know I planned on coming back to you. I told you the day I left that I would be back."

Oh, hell no. She felt the anger come back until she was sure she'd choke. "I never thought it would be almost sixteen years later, Devon. I thought you were just going to the fucking store or something! You said, "I'll be back," and kissed me goodbye. I was so drugged up on pain meds, I didn't even barely remember you telling me.

"For the first two years, I hardly left your mother's house. You never called, never even wrote. What in the hell was I supposed to think?"

"I'm sorry, Sarah. I am. Please, you have to forgive me. I'll make it up to you, I promise."

"You left me at the most crucial time in my life. I needed you, and you disappeared. You can't make that time up."

"I was just as heartbroken as you, Sarah. Never think that I didn't mourn the loss of our child. I still do, every day! You don't think I wonder what he or she would have looked like? I can't even come close to children without feeling the pain of our loss. You weren't the only one alone. If I would have stayed here, they would have found me and forced me to leave. That would have put you and my mother at risk. We'd just lost the baby. I couldn't lose anyone else!"

Sarah pushed herself off the floor to stand. "You could have left a note explaining things instead of leaving me to worry about whether or not you were even alive."

"Would you have believed a note?"

She watched him walk over to her until only inches separated them. "No, probably not, but at least it would be something. All your mother and I knew was that you had left."

Fingertips traced down her jaw line, and all remnants of the devastating thoughts vanished. Something strange stirred in her insides until she rested her palms against his hard, wide chest so she wouldn't mold her body against his. Deep down, she hated not being able to control herself.

"Sarah, don't fight the way you feel." His hands ran up her back, pulling her closer. "I love you. Please tell me a part of you is still open to loving me back."

She quickly pulled away. Isn't this what she spent years trying to avoid? Opening herself up to Gavin was one thing. He'd never hurt her, She could feel it. Devon on the other hand had.

"I can't do this right now. It's too much. I'll keep your secret, but I have to go."

Sarah quickly ran out of the apartment and back toward her own before he could stop her. She was surprised to see Gavin standing at her door with flowers. Once again, he'd come back. She couldn't help but love his perfect timing. The last thing she wanted to think about was what she just learned. Gavin could help her with that.

Chapter 7

"I couldn't leave. I'm sorry. I thought I'd take you up on your offer to stay over."

Sarah nodded, and turned back to see Devon standing at his door. All he was wearing was a pair of shorts. The built of his body combined with the expression on his face caused her to turn away before she was tempted to stare longer. She quickly pulled the irresistible blond inside her apartment. "I'm glad." She inhaled the roses deeply and tried to smile. "Thank you, they're beautiful."

"Are you all right? You've been crying. Did you learn what happened with…Devon?"

Taking the flowers from him, she made her way to the table, placing them in the vase. She nodded at him as she headed over to fill it with water. When she reached the table, she finally looked up.

"Yes, he told me."

"And you're sure you're okay?"

"I will be, I think." Walking over to the couch, she waited for Gavin to sit down, but he didn't.

"And he told you what he is?"

She narrowed her eyes at him, not sure if he meant what she thought he did, and she wasn't about to risk Devon's secret. She might be angry with her ex at the moment, but she'd never betray him no matter what happened in their past.

"I'm not sure what you mean."

Gavin smiled. "You're getting defensive. I can feel it. I can tell he told you. You're taking the news of what we are rather well. But I knew you would."

"You're a...a..." Sarah couldn't get the word out of her mouth. So, that's what they were talking in code about earlier.

"Werewolf, yes. Your...ex is afraid I'll mark you as my mate, but I wasn't about to do that until you knew and consented. To be marked by a werewolf has its pleasures and pains. For one, we'd never really be able to be apart. It would cause us physical pain much like now, but worse. As for the pleasures, well," he laughed, "someday maybe we'll find out that part."

"And..." she recalled the conversation earlier, "Ayden, he's one too?"

"Yes, he's alpha for this area. Every major city has one. Houston, Austin, Dallas...Waco."

Trying to process all the information, she placed her head in her palms. How was it that no one knew werewolves existed? By the sound of it, they weren't anywhere near extinct.

"Wait." Sarah brought up her head to look at him. "Oh god, Stephen and Brandon are friends with Ayden. And what about Trevor? I'm assuming he's one, too."

"Trevor is., As for Stephen, the name rings a bell, but it's a pretty common name. If you're talking about the Brandon I think you're talking about, then no, he's not a wolf."

"Well, the Brandon I know has dark hair, very pale, with the most gorgeous eyes. He's one of my friend Evelyn's boyfriends."

"Vampire, not werewolf. And I've heard about that couple. It was a first actually, vampire, werewolf, and human. Remarkable, if I say so myself."

"Vampire," Sarah whispered. If she wasn't shocked before, she sure the hell was now. "If you tell me there are such things as mermaids, I think I'll go into a shock induced coma. Vampire!"

Gavin laughed, pulling her into his lap on the couch. "Not that I'm aware of, but I wouldn't be surprised."

"Don't say that. Just hold me."

The warmth felt so inviting Sarah snuggled into his chest. He smelled of the ocean and spring, all wrapped into one. Something about him calmed her and promised she'd never hurt again. She wanted more than anything to believe that, but the fresh pain from tonight told her otherwise.

"Gavin," she looked up, "the way I feel with you, is it because of what you are? Because I promise, this is totally out of character for me. I don't do relationships. At all."

He smiled and kissed her forehead. "Yes, but only true mates are supposed to feel like this. It was nearly impossible for me to leave earlier. I didn't even make it back to the motel before I had to turn around and come back. And the bad thing is I haven't even marked you yet."

"Is it possible for two people to be drawn to one individual?" She tried to think of a different way to word it. "Can two males mark a mate?"

"I'm sure it's possible, but rarely heard of. Why?"

"Just wondering, that's all."

Gavin's lips found hers, and she kissed him hungrily. The couch pressed against her back the moment he lowered her down, covering her with his weight. She moaned at the hardness that pressed against her pussy. Wetness quickly soaked into her panties.

Desperate to feel more of him, Sarah pulled off his shirt, running her hands down the smooth expanse of his chest. Breathing heavily, Gavin broke their kiss just as it started heating back up.

"This isn't why I came back. You know that, right?"

"Yes, but I'm glad you did. I didn't want to be alone."

"Sarah, do you think maybe I shouldn't have come back? I don't want you to feel like I'm rushing an already rushed situation, but we have so much we need to discuss."

"Don't leave, please. You're right. We do need to talk, but not right now. Touch me, Gavin. Let me feel your cock inside of me. You feel so good."

His lips crushed hers again as buttons flew from her flannel shirt. The cool air brushed against her skin, making her shiver. The immediate warmth of his hand on the outside of her lace bra penetrated heat to her core. Her nipples pushed against the lace, almost painfully.

"Fuck me, Gavin." She whispered the words into her ear, feeling his groan vibrate all the way to her clit.

Sarah was lifted so abruptly she didn't realize she was even off the couch until they entered her room. She reached down, unbuttoning his pants just as they came to the bed. In one swift motion, he pulled her pants off. The sound of the ripped jean material turned her on more than she thought possible. The amount of strength he was capable of amazed her.

"God, your scent is so strong. I love the way you smell."

Gavin kicked off his pants, pressing his completely nude body against hers. The need to take off her undergarments and feel his skin completely on hers drove her crazy. Like a slap in the face, Devon's face appeared behind her closed lids. Angrily, she blocked it and tried to focus on Gavin.

He lifted, looking at her. "What was that? I felt... pushed. Did you want me to stop?"

Startled at how clearly he could feel her emotions, she shook her head. "No, don't stop. It was nothing." She quickly used the opportunity to take off her bra. He smiled and slowly pulled down her panties.

"Geez, this is tough."

"What is?" Sarah asked, reaching for him.

"This pull we have. I know it'll get better after you're marked, but I've never experienced anything like this. It's like I can't get enough of the way you smell, feel, taste..." He closed his eyes, inhaling deeply. When his eyes opened, Sarah noticed the color once again turned darker.

"Is the mark painful?"

"No, not that I've heard."

Sarah pulled him back on top of her body, basking in the feel of his skin when there was a knock at the door. They both paused and looked at each other.

"Are you expecting anyone?" Gavin slid his pants on while Sarah threw on her robe.

"No. All my friends are probably out. It's Saturday night."

They both entered the living room as a knock sounded so loud Sarah almost screamed. Her door literally shook from the amount of force used.

Gavin held up his hand to make sure she didn't move and opened the door. She wanted to curse when she saw Devon, but the look on his face quickly made her heart rate escalated. It wasn't anger, but panic.

"What happened?" Sarah quickly approached the door.

"It's what's happening that I don't like." The warning in his voice washed away the anxiety replacing it with rage.

A ragged breath came out of her mouth as she wrapped her arms around her waist. "Devon, I really don't think it's any of your business what's going on over here. Gavin is staying. If you don't like it, then I don't know what to tell you. Geez, I freaking thought something happened, *an emergency.*"

"It very well might be. Tell me why you want him to stay. Is it because of what happened between us earlier? You can't help the way you feel, Sarah. Don't try to ignore it."

"Don't tell me how I fucking feel, Devon. Gavin's here because I want him here, and he's not going anywhere. Ever." There it was. That possessiveness was creeping back in. Screw it. It was the truth. She suddenly didn't care if he ever left.

"What happened earlier?" Gavin asked, looking toward her.

"It's nothing," she said angrily.

Devon laughed. "Oh, I wouldn't agree. We were meant to be together, Sarah. We always have been. If you fight the pull, it's only going to get stronger."

"Impossible," Gavin whispered. He slowly turned to Devon. "I'm afraid we might have a problem then because she's meant to be mated to me."

"What in the hell are you talking about?" Devon snapped his gaze toward Gavin.

"You may have been alpha, but that doesn't make me stupid. I know what I feel, and she'll tell you how she feels. The bonding has already started, and it's getting stronger. I promised I wouldn't mark her until she's consented. How long do you think that will take? We already can't stand to be separated."

"I told you what I would do if your teeth came anywhere close to her," Devon said angrily. "I've loved her for more years than the hours you've known her. If anyone has a right to mark her, it's me. Besides, you *can* be separated. If it were impossible, I wouldn't have been able to leave. It hurts like hell, but you won't die." Devon paused, studying Gavin. "At first, I thought you might mark her just to be a prick, but this whole *we're all three bonding* just takes the cake. You're fucking amazing, you know that?"

"Oh, I assure you it's the truth. For all I know, you're the liar."

Both men closed in on each other. From the look of fury clearly expressed by their tense bodies, Sarah had no doubt things were about to get bad. "Stop it, both of you. No one is marking me anytime soon, so there's no point in arguing."

Gavin tore his gaze from Devon and surprised Sarah by smiling. His hands cupped her face. "May I kiss you and demonstrate what we share?"

She nodded, feeling extremely uncomfortable. The moment her new lover's lips brushed hers, she could feel herself pulling his body closer. He broke the kiss breathing heavily and turned to Devon. "Go near her. I want to see just how powerful your pull is. Sarah, is that all right? It's just a test. You can stop it whenever you want."

Nervously, she looked back and forth between the two of them. "No, I…can't."

Devon took a step toward her. "Sarah, please. Gavin obviously isn't lying about the two of you. I could feel your connection. But I know I'm not imagining what we share. If the pull isn't there, then I'll leave, but I have to know."

Could she do this? Would getting close to Devon affect her the way Gavin did? She knew it would! But she needed to know just how much. If for some reason it didn't, maybe they both could move on. And that meant no more interruptions.

He stood there with his hand outstretched. Gavin walked beside her, nodding to her it was okay. Sarah placed her fingers through her ex's and stepped forward against his body. The tidal wave of emotions left her breathless. She looked into Devon's gray eyes and saw his head lowering. For the life of her, she couldn't turn away. She didn't want to.

The first brush of his full lips sent electricity coursing through her body, but she remained still, trying her best to not give in to the temptation. He ran his tongue between her lips, leaving a trail of wetness. A shiver raced through her. Instantly, her body reacted on its own. She could feel her arms wrapping around his neck, pulling him forward. The taste erupted over every inch as her tongued dueled with his. And suddenly, he was gone.

Sarah opened her eyes to see Devon clear across the room. They stood almost in the hallway, and Gavin held her against his body. "All right, so we have a problem," he was saying, but his words sounded distorted, far away. There was only one thing she knew, and that was that she wanted both of them fucking her senseless, right now.

"Oh shit," she said breathlessly.

"Yeah, we do have a problem. So, what do we do about it? I can tell you one thing, you're not staying here," Devon said, walking forward.

Sarah clutched the arms around her even tighter, afraid she would run back to her ex if he came any closer, but she wasn't about to let him start giving orders in her house. "Devon, you can't tell me who stays or who goes. I make the decision, and I don't want to be alone, so he stays."

"Well, if he stays, then so do I. No offense, Gavin, but I don't trust you not marking her. She's obviously trying to bond to both of us. We'll just have to figure something out."

"Ugh, Devon that is so not fair." Sarah ripped herself away from Gavin and stalked toward him. "Why are you making this hard?"

She stood directly in front of him, breathing heavily. Devon's face turned from angry to sad within seconds. Seeing him get upset made her clutch her chest from the ache she felt.

"I love you, Sarah. And I know you still love me. Don't rush into something without searching your true feelings. Take your time to really get to know me and…Gavin. I think you'll find we're not the people who you think we are. I've changed, and you just met this person. Do you even know what he does for a living? How old is he? What are his favorite things to do? What about favorite foods? Think about it, the bond is blinding you from anything but sexual tendencies."

Stunned, she turned toward the gorgeous blond. "Oh god, he's right. I don't know anything about you. Just like, you don't know anything about me. Devon…I don't know what to do. I can't think."

Large arms wrapped around her, pulling her close while she tried to clear her head. Maybe it was better if she wasn't around either one of them.

"Gavin can stay with me. I know how hard it is for everyone involved to be separated. Tomorrow, we'll all sit down and get to know each other better. Shit, Sarah, I don't even know what you do for a living."

Looking up at Devon, she smiled. "I'm a real estate agent, and pretty successful if I do say so myself."

"Of course you are." He laughed. "Who wouldn't want to buy anything you were trying to sell. I think I'd by ten houses just to get your attention." He paused and then hugged her tightly to him. The nearness made her tense. Sexual tendencies or not, she still wasn't sure she was okay with Devon being back in her life.

"All right, Gavin. Let's go back to my place. You can stay until we get this matter resolved."

Hesitantly, he walked over. Sarah went into his arms while he hugged and kissed her goodbye. Sadly and utterly confused, she watched them both leave. The depressing silence of her apartment nagged at her. How in the hell did she manage to get herself into this mess? Two men, werewolves at that, were trying to bond with her. Which one would she choose?

She would never have considered herself stupid. She thought back to when Brandon and Stephen approached her about Evelyn. They wanted to know what to do about their situation, and what did she tell them? *"Why should she have to choose? Grow up. You two get along and make her happy."* True, she was sure they already thought of that on their own and only wanted her acceptance without her knowing it, but still, it seemed to be working for them.

There was only one problem. Could she forgive the man who'd broken her heart? She'd always dreamed he'd come back. As much anger as she harbored for him, she couldn't lie to herself and say her love had disappeared. It hadn't. But would he leave again? Could she trust him? Maybe. Deep down, she knew she wanted to. It was time to get some advice.

A smile formed across her face. Sarah didn't waste any time as she ran to her phone. It was time she made a call to someone with experience in this situation, someone who had their own paranormal relationship in full swing.

Chapter 8

Sarah looked at the clock and cringed. It was a little after ten. She prayed Evelyn was either getting ready to go out or was awake. The thought that she was waking anyone up didn't sit well with her. Of course, if she knew those guys, they were far from being asleep.

"Hello?" Evelyn said, a little out of breath.

"Please tell me you're not doing what I think you're doing."

"No." She laughed. "We're watching movies over here at Nicole's. I almost didn't get to my phone in time. What's up?"

Sarah sighed, relieved. "I have a problem, and you're the only one who can help me."

"What's wrong? Hold on. Let me go outside so I can hear you. The sound of rustling and noise quickly turned to silence. "Okay, now what's going on?"

"Devon and Gavin. Need I say more? I left with Gavin, the blond from last night and something happened between us. Oh god, Evelyn he's wonderful. I haven't felt this good in years." Sarah quickly got control over her softening voice. "But that's not the problem, Devon and I also have this pull and….oh wait, I forgot the major thing. Yeah, they're werewolves. Thanks for giving me a heads-up that they even exist, Ev!"

"Oh, shit. I can't tell you those sorts of things, Sarah. But now that you know, you say you're pulling to both of them? Like, really pulling to bond or just attraction? How strong is the pull?"

"Let's just say after everything Devon and I have been through, I was still ready to throw myself at him the moment his lips touched mine. I've never felt anything like this before. And, with Gavin, it's just as strong. We can't be apart from each other for very long without us both feeling it. And truthfully, I don't ever want to let him go. The thought is inconceivable."

"Well, shit, I'm with a vampire and a werewolf so I don't know much, but hold on. I know someone who is bonded to two werewolves." The sound of the door opening was quickly followed by the shout for Nicole.

Sarah listened to Evelyn relay over the information. A soft voice got on the phone. "Hello, this is Nicole."

"Hi, I'm Sarah. I think we've met a time or two. What do I do about my situation? I feel lost. There are so many problems between the three of us, and I don't know where to start."

"Well, take it from me, when you're feeling the pull there is nothing you can do to prevent it. It'll always be there, so I'd advise you to just go with it. I know Devon. We met when he first arrived in town. Since he was alpha in Waco, he had to clear things with Ayden and promise not to try to take over for this area. I immediately liked him. He seems like a good guy. Now Gavin, on the other hand, I've only met briefly, but I liked him, too."

"So, you're telling me if I'm pulling to both of them, the feeling is never going to go away?"

"Exactly. If I were you, I'd start making them get along or else you're in for a bumpy ride. Face it, Sarah, you're in the same boat as Ev and I. Might as well grab your men and come eat popcorn and watch a movie with us. Welcome to the club."

Evelyn's laugh echoed through the phone as she got back on. "Yay for Sarah! Well, now that you have two boyfriends, too, I guess we'll be hanging out more. No more Bets for you."

Sarah took a deep breath. "So how do I get them to get along? Gavin's already spending the night at Devon's, three damn doors down from my apartment. Devon doesn't trust him not to mark me, so they're shacked up."

"Leave them there together for as long as you can. I noticed the more time Brandon and Stephen hung out together, the more they got along. Now, don't separate them. The bond the three of you will grow will be impenetrable. You'll see. I've never been happier."

"Thanks, Ev. I don't think we're quite ready for movie night at Club Ménage, but give it a few weeks and I'm sure we'll fit right in."

"Club Ménage, I like that. Brandon will, too. Okay, take care, sweetie. If you need anything, let me know."

"Will do, love you, Ev."

Sarah tossed the phone on the bedside table the moment she walked into the room. So, the key was to leave them alone. Great, what did that do for her? How would she manage?

Come on, Sarah. You've been alone for how long now? It's time you got back on your usual schedule. You've never needed a man to feel complete. Don't start now.

Crawling into bed after what she just experienced with both of the men made her feel even more alone, but she closed her eyes and willed herself to fall asleep. It wasn't long before unconsciousness took over, and she was out.

* * * *

Gavin grabbed his bag out of his car and followed Devon inside. Uncomfortable, didn't even begin to describe the way he felt. The sound of his bags falling to the floor was the only thing that broke the silence.

Slowly, he walked forward, taking in all of the pictures. The state of his emotions flared as he looked around. So many memories covered the walls. They shared so much pain and pleasure, and all he had was a few amazing hours with Sarah. How in the hell could he compete?

"I knew you loved her, but I didn't know you loved her this much."

Devon laughed from behind him. "I've always felt that way for her, from the moment I heard her laugh coming down the school hallway. My first day didn't go so well at the new school, but when I found her, nothing else matter. We were inseparable from our freshman year until I had to leave. I've never felt pain like losing Sarah…or the baby."

"I don't want to lose her either. I know you share a lot, but I just can't imagine being away from her for long. Can I ask you a question, Devon?"

Devon sat down on the couch. "It depends. What do you want to know?"

"Why didn't you mark her when you were together before?"

Devon put his head in his hands and rubbed his eyes. "I just thought it was something I would share with her when we got married. Don't get me wrong, I wanted to, badly, but it didn't seem right at the time. Maybe I knew something big was about to happen. I don't know."

Gavin nodded, walking over to a bookshelf full of pictures. One hid behind the others. He pulled it out, examining the small five-by-seven picture. Sarah stood there, smiling, molding her light blue T-shirt to her stomach. The signs of her pregnancy weren't really evident, but he had no doubt that she was carrying Devon's child. The heartache coming directly from behind him caused Gavin to stiffen. He never even heard Devon move in to look.

The picture disappeared from his hands. "Why don't you take your things to the room?" Devon placed the picture back and walked into the kitchen. Gavin wasn't about to argue with the alpha, he complied.

* * * *

Devon fought the pain racing through his chest. Why had coming back made everything so much more intense? In Waco it hurt, but it was manageable. Here, so close to Sarah, he could feel the pull down to his toes. The urge to knock on her door and beg her forgiveness ate away at his insides.

The love they once shared never wavered on his end. He loved her so much more than he did when he left this place to begin with. What could he do to make her love him back, to forgive him for what he'd done?

And what about this new guy? He couldn't just let the guy go through the rest of his life in pain for not having his mate. Devon was alpha, meant to protect and take care of pack, and even though he wasn't in charge of this territory, he still felt the need to protect Gavin from the pain. He hated feeling compassion for the same man who wanted Sarah. But ultimately, he couldn't help it.

Pouring himself a cup of coffee, he stared out the kitchen window into the lit up parking lot. This was so different than the ranch. It would take a while to get used to the noise and the lights, but he'd do it again. Sarah was worth any cost. He just regretted not being able to come back sooner.

Waco, of course, had been out of the question for her. He couldn't have been by her side at all times, and that's what it would have taken. With the way those wolves were, they wouldn't have thought twice to use her as a way to get back at him. Even up until the day he left things were chaotic. It was a pure miracle that he'd found the new alpha when he did.

The sound of footsteps echoed behind him. Slowly, he turned to look at Gavin's face from across the room. Damn, this was going to be hard. Too many conflicting emotions ran through him. Did he offer the guy the bed, or did he beat the crap out of him to prove who the better man for Sarah was? Sometimes being an alpha wasn't anything but trouble.

"I'm not really tired. Why don't you take the bed tonight? I'm going to sit up and watch TV for a while."

Gavin gave him a half smile. "I'm not tired, either."

Devon sat on one side of the couch while Gavin sat at the other. Turning on ESPN, both remained quiet for a long time. The first mention of baseball, and Devon almost forgot about the other man sitting on his sofa.

"Oh, come on! Dammit! I can't believe the Braves lost." Tightening his grip around the remote, Devon had to make sure he didn't throw the damn thing towards the television.

"I don't know the first thing about baseball, but when football season starts, you bet your ass I'll be watching the games," Gavin said, looking back at the TV.

"Let me guess. You're a Cowboys fan?" Devon said sarcastically.

Gavin looked over and smiled. "That should be my line, *cowboy*. No, I'm not partial to the team."

"Very funny, city boy. So who do you follow if you're not a Dallas fan?"

"I don't follow teams. I follow players. Now Adrian Peterson, he's someone to follow."

Devon laughed. "Yeah, he's okay I guess, but what about Cedric Benson? Now he really ripped up the football field, didn't he? I've followed him since he was a sophomore in Midland."

"Well, at least we agree on sports. As for anything else, that is yet to be determined."

Devon looked back to the TV, not furthering the conversation. The last thing he wanted was to like this guy. He needed to remember that Gavin was also somewhat competing with him for Sarah, although he wasn't sure how that was going to work out. Regardless of what either one of them wanted, if he was right, then they'd all be stuck together for a very long time.

Chapter 9

Sarah woke up to the smell of bacon heavily drifting in the air. She sat up confused. Her hair hung in knotted waves around her face. Sleepily, she turned to look at the clock and fell back against her pillow. *Seven freaking o'clock, and someone is in my kitchen cooking breakfast. Which one is it? And how in the hell did they get in my house?*

Sighing, she threw back the covers and crawled out of bed. The robe she still had on was twisted, exposing the whole right side of her body. She quickly fixed it and looked up to see Devon standing in her doorway.

"I thought I heard you awake. Gavin and I are making breakfast. Coffee?"

Sarah couldn't ignore the heat blazing in his eyes. Her insides responded immediately. A part of her hated how the bond was pushing her to forgive him faster than she wanted to.

"Yes, lots and lots of coffee."

Walking forward, she waited for him to move so she could get by. When he didn't, she looked up.

"I always loved the way you looked first thing in the morning. I can still remember you curled up in my twin size bed at my moms. You know, she still has that bed."

"Does, she? Well, I guess it was good my parents kicked me out when they...did, or else you would have never seen me in such a mess." Damn, she was about to say pregnant, but the word just wouldn't come out.

Devon laughed and kissed her forehead, moving only slightly out of the way. The tips of her breasts brushed against his lower chest while she scooted past. Her nipples tightened in response, and the beginning of a moan past her lips. It took everything for her to continue to the living room. The urge to pull him back to her bed unnerved her. Fuck, her pussy was so wet at the thought of his cock pounding into her.

Evelyn and Nicole might be right, but she wasn't giving into anything so soon. Devon was right on one thing. She needed to get to know them both better, and she had every intention of doing that as soon as possible.

"Smells good," Sarah said, walking into the kitchen. Grabbing a coffee cup, she poured and leaned against the counter.

"So whose brilliant idea was it to surprise me with breakfast?"

Gavin turned to look toward Devon, who walked in and sat down at the table. "Mine. I know how breakfast used to be your favorite meal."

Sarah looked toward her ex. "I haven't eaten breakfast since you left," she whispered.

Knots filled her stomach. Facing the past wasn't going to be easy. The thought downright terrified her. Between the memories of waking up next to Devon and now this, it was too much, too soon. "But you're back so I guess this is the perfect way to start the day. Excuse me."

Placing the coffee cup down, Sarah walked toward her room fighting the tears that threatened to spill over. So much anger and hurt filled her. Recalling the days she spent in that same damn twin size bed crying for someone who never came back rubbed her heart raw.

"Sarah. Please."

She turned around in her room to see Devon standing not a foot away. "What? I'm just getting dressed?"

"No, that's not why you came in here. I hurt your feelings by bringing up the past. Come here." Sarah didn't move even though she wanted to. "Sarah, please. I just want to hold you, nothing more."

Slowly, she walked into his arms. Calmness filled her the moment she felt the heat from his body. She could feel herself relaxing and peace taking over. This was the way she wanted to feel, but she wasn't so sure it was ever going to be possible.

"Better?"

She nodded as he walked her back into the kitchen. Gavin looked at her concerned but gave her a tender smile. "How do you like your eggs, scrambled or over easy?"

"Scrambled." Sarah grabbed her coffee cup and sat back down at the table.

"I want mine over easy." Devon smiled toward him.

Sarah looked back and forth. The tension thickened in the air. Dammit, she prayed they weren't starting already.

"You can make your own damn eggs. I'm only making these for her."

"All right, all right, no need to get your panties in a wad, city boy."

Something passed through Gavin. First he tensed, but almost instantly relaxed. He laughed and winked, surprising the shit out of her. "Did you know ol' Devon over here is a Braves fan? I told him the Red Sox are better, but he doesn't want to listen."

Sarah laughed at the odd subject, but decided to play along. She knew he was just trying to ease their odd situation. "Well, I happen to be a Yankees fan. Derek Jeter is dreamy, isn't he?"

Devon busted out laughing, and Gavin narrowed his eyes and turned off the stove. "Did you hear that Devon? I think our girl Sarah just said she was a Yankees fan."

"Oh, I heard all right? The question is what are we going to do about it?"

"What?" Sarah asked, smiling. "If you want to talk sports, then you've come to the right place. I can name the hottest guys from every team, in every sport."

"Is that right?" Gavin said, coming to the table. "Name your favorite college football team."

Sarah laughed, rolling her eyes. "Devon, help him out. Who's always been my favorite?"

"UT, of course." She watched him smile, and she turned back in the direction of the gorgeous guy quizzing her.

"Player," Gavin said, raising his eyebrow.

"Colt McCoy, of course."

"NFL?"

"Now this one's harder. So many hotties." She laughed.

"Devon," Gavin said, inching closer to her.

"Oh, I know. She's getting herself in a load of trouble, but let's hear what she has to say."

Sarah bit her lip, pretending to think. "Well, I'll skip all the others and just name the hottest. I wouldn't want your breakfasts to get cold. I'd have to say Tom Brady for the Patriots. I swear if he ever needs to buy a house down here, I'll…"

Sarah squealed as both Devon and Gavin picked her up, tickling her. She felt as the men shuffled back quite a few steps. As they came into the living room, they didn't stay standing for long. With her twisting and jerking against their hold they lowered her to the carpet.

Gavin was lying between her thighs while Devon wrapped around her from behind. Their hands seemed to be everywhere. Even though she laughed to the point she couldn't breathe, their touch was causing more sensations than just tickling. Sarah took a deep breath as Devon's hands froze on the sides of her breasts. Gavin's hands stopped completely, just under them.

"Your scent." Gavin closed his eyes, inhaling deeply. Gavin's fingers held firm to the sides of her ribs as he lowered his head to the bottom of her stomach. She moaned, leaning farther back against the hardness of Devon's body behind her.

"No," Devon snapped. "Sarah, I think you should get dressed. We all need to clear our heads. Let's go, city boy."

Gavin looked up, his eyes a deep green. "Devon, I don't see why you fight it. I know you want her as much as I do. I can feel it. Plus, Sarah wants both of us whether we like it or not. Now, we just have to figure out what to do about it I sure as hell don't plan on giving her up, and I know you don't either."

"You got that right," Devon growled. "But I sure as hell am not ready to share her either."

Sarah sighed, and wiggled her way out from under both of them. "Thanks for breakfast. I'll grab a plate before I leave. You two better figure out how you're going to work things out. I've got a few busy weeks ahead of me so when you see me I don't want you two fighting. Gavin's right. We're all in this together, and there's nothing we can do about it. Now, you both go so I can get dressed. I have an appointment I need to go to."

"An appointment? On a Sunday?"

Sarah looked toward Gavin. "Yes, if you must know. Sylvia comes in on Sundays to do my hair and my nails, *and* I have a date with my girls. That's not a problem, is it?"

"No, of course not," he said quietly. Devon just smiled at her change of mood.

"Good, now off with you two. I'll see you for dinner. And I'm cooking. Six o'clock and don't be late or else I lock the door and eat by myself."

She tried not to laugh at how bossy she sounded, but if she truly wanted to get back to her old self and try not getting hurt in the process, it was the only way.

"See you tonight, sweetheart. Have fun," Devon said, practically pulling Gavin out of the door.

A cry of frustration bounced off the walls while she walked to her room to get dressed. Damn, that was a close one. Being sandwiched between those two bodies drove her insides crazy. She would have gladly fucked both of them right there on the floor if it wasn't for Devon. At least he showed restraint. She somehow needed to convince herself to take things slow, but patient was something she'd never been.

* * * *

Devon pushed Gavin inside his apartment and narrowed his eyes angrily. "What in the hell do you think you were doing? Are you fucking serious? You're not in the city anymore. You treat Sarah with respect, or I'll make you. Don't use the bond we all have together as some excuse to fuck her any chance you get."

Gavin instantly slammed his fist into Devon's face. "For one, quit calling me city boy, I have a fucking name. It's Gavin. And for your information, I'm not using the tie we all have as an excuse to get some ass like you think. I have control. If you didn't notice from her scent, she wanted both of us. I was just trying to please her. That's what caring for someone is all about. Do you seriously think I'd want to pleasure her in front of you! Hell no. But I will if it makes her happy.

"And another thing, Devon," Gavin said, spitting out his name. "Just so you know, I feel what Sarah feels. She wants so badly to forgive you and move things along, but you're going to end up ruining it for all of us. You're cocky, arrogant, and you think you know what she wants. I've known her for a fraction of the time you have, and I can see you know nothing of what makes Sarah the person she is."

Devon rubbed his jaw and stared at the younger man in stunned silence. The urge to knock this punk on his ass was strong, but the truth Gavin spoke hit him like a brick.

"She wants to forgive me?"

Gavin took a step back and breathed heavily. "She loves you more than you'll ever know. But you hurt her badly. I felt it the night we met. Sarah's damaged inside, but I think if we work on it together, we'll be able to mend what you broke."

Devon wasn't sure what to think. The last thing he wanted to do involved sharing Sarah, but was that what she really wanted? And would he be able to actually go through with it?"

Chapter 10

All day, Gavin watched the hours painfully tick away. Sarah expected them over in fifteen minutes, and it felt like there were hours to go. Being separated from her all day quickly became torture after the first ninety minutes. Without the mark in place, he'd continue to feel this way. How much time would go by before they all could agree and he and Devon could tie her to them forever?

The tall cowboy continued to pace, although today he didn't look much like a cowboy. He wore tight wranglers and boots, but instead of the hat or western shirt he had worn in the past, he now sported a tucked in white T-shirt.

As Devon tried to control his nervousness, Gavin studied his frame. All alphas usually were wide, but the height was new. The tallest alpha he'd seen was Ayden, and he was only an inch shorter than the cowboy. But Devon's six foot five inch height made Gavin feel small, and he was six feet two inches.

"Hey, Devon, sit down. You're making me nervous."

A glare was directed at him, but Devon listened. "Hell, I *am* nervous. This little plan you came up with better work. I don't like it, but if it'll make Sarah happy, then I want to try."

"It'll work. Just remember, I'm doing this for all of us. If I find out you're trying to take Sarah away from me somehow, past alpha or not, I *will* kick your ass."

Devon laughed. "Gavin, if Sarah wants you, then nothing I try is going to be able to change the pull or her mind. I'm not sure which one is stronger. When Sarah wants something, she gets it. You'll see."

"Do you know how hard this is going to be for me? Leaving her alone with you is bad enough, but leaving her period is the hardest. I've missed her all day. Now, I finally get to see her at dinner and then I'm gone. I don't like it, but it's the only way I know to move things forward. *You* set us back. Everything was fine until you freaked out this morning."

"Okay, shit! I've heard this all day. Enough, already."

Gavin looked at the clock and sighed. Ten more minutes and he'd finally be able to see her. Devon started to stand, but the look he gave him had Devon rolling his eyes and leaning forward instead. Damn, the day lingered on forever, and now he'd be alone tonight. Well, he'd make the best of the time with Sarah as he could.

* * * *

Sarah opened the oven and rolled her eyes. Picking up the cookbook, she thrummed through the pages. The instructions did say bake a little over an hour, right? Surely, she hadn't taken more than two hours to get dressed. Well, she did take her time in the shower, and then fixing her hair. Oh, and the clothes. Quickly, she scanned the words.

"Bake at three hundred fifty degrees for one and a half hours, basting every thirty minutes." Sarah paused. "Basting every thirty minutes? Dammit! How did I miss that part?" She looked back toward the dry, burnt rosemary chicken she'd worked so hard on preparing. "Well, fuck. What in the hell do I do now?"

A knock made her look up. She quickly laid the book down and wiped her hands on the new white apron she'd bought. Sarah had spent so much time at the grocery store, she completely missed lunch with her girls. Melissa didn't mind calling and teasing her terribly for trying to make dinner.

Taking a quick peek at herself in the mirror, she took in her reflection—black slacks, red silk blouse with her blonde hair in waves. Damn, she looked like Christmas. Well, it was too late to change now.

As Sarah reached for the knob she hesitated. Fear like nothing she felt before exploded inside of her, leaving her body shaking as she began to back away. Her mind was screaming to run, but already entering the kitchen, there was nowhere to go.

The sound of wood cracking as someone's fist pounded into the door made her cover her mouth to hold in a scream. Who in the hell would be banging like that? For some reason, she knew it wasn't Devon or Gavin.

A ring echoed through the living room. "Shit," she whispered, running to her purse. The moment she hit the ignore button the door crashed to the floor. Air rushed against Sarah's face, blowing her hair back at the force of the fall. She couldn't move as she stood there staring at Tom. Their gazes locked, and time seemed to slow in her fear.

"Sarah!"

Devon's voice in the background only registered briefly. All she could see were Tom's eyes glaring at her before he disappeared. The adrenaline hit so hard and so fast Sarah collapsed to the ground breathing heavily. Seconds hadn't gone by when she noticed Gavin kneeling next to her.

"Are you all right? Was that the guy who's been calling?"

Shakily, Sarah nodded. "Where's Devon?" She immediately stood. Her legs shaking almost made it impossible.

"He ran after the guy."

"Why didn't you go with him?" she said frantically.

"He told me to stay with you. Do you know how strong he is? He wouldn't have needed me for one guy. Sarah, he's an alpha. The guy wouldn't stand a chance against Devon."

Walking to the door, she peeked out, not seeing anything. "Gavin, if something happens to him…"

He quickly embraced her in his arms. "He'll be all right. Shh... It's okay."

Sarah couldn't think. "I just got him back. If I lost him again, I'm not sure what would happen to me."

Gavin stroked his fingers through her hair while he made soothing sounds and pulled her deeper into the living room. Nausea threatened at the thoughts of any harm befalling the one man she tried endlessly to forget. Suddenly, she didn't want to have him missing from her anymore. Even if she hadn't completely forgiven him, she didn't want him gone either.

The sound of footsteps had Sarah spinning around. Devon walked through the door slowly, and she ran, throwing herself into his arms. "He had a car waiting by. I couldn't keep up with him, but I did get the license plate number."

"Why did you do that? You could have gotten hurt." The sobs wracked her chest as she fought to breathe against the panic flaring inside of her.

"Whoa, honey, calm down. I'm fine. Don't cry. Here let me see." Devon lifted her face up, wiping the tears away with his thumb. "Are you okay?"

Was she okay? Fuck no, she wasn't okay. One minute she was confused, and the next, she was ready to pledge her undying love to the one man she thought she'd never forgive. That shit wasn't normal.

"Yes, I'm fine. He didn't do anything besides bang my door down, but you shouldn't have gone after him. It could have been dangerous."

"You let me worry about danger. I'm just glad you're all right. If I wouldn't have heard the loud knocking..." Devon tensed against her. He held her tighter, resting his head down on hers.

Recalling the banging, Sarah looked at her door. "Now how in the hell am I supposed to explain that to the manager? She's going to flip. I think he broke the frame."

Devon looked at her, shocked. "Someone tried to break into your house, and you're worried about the damn door? Sarah, you could have been hurt. You have no idea who that guy was. He could have been a murderer, a rapist. Do you know how lucky you are?"

Turning to Gavin, she wasn't sure what to say. Devon didn't give her time to do anything. "Gavin, do you know something you're not telling me? You both are looking at each other like you're hiding something."

"We're not hiding anything. Sarah told me she knows who it is."

"Well, who the hell is it then?"

Confused on how to start, she quickly pulled away and sat down on the couch. "If you fix my door, I'll tell you everything, the whole story. You're both going to find out anyway."

"Wait, there's more? I thought he was just some random guy you saw once and brushed off. Isn't that what you said?"

She looked at Gavin, twisting her mouth. "Yes, that's what I said, and it's true, but there's more to it than just that. If you at least try to fix my door, I'll tell you. I don't like it being open. I feel exposed."

Her ex sniffed the air, and a smile began to appear on his face. The look he gave her caused Sarah to roll her eyes. She knew what was coming.

"Hey, is something burning?" Devon walked into the kitchen and laughed.

"You know very well I could never cook. I might have left it in there too long, and well, I missed the part in the instructions where it said you had to baste every thirty minutes. I plan to do better tomorrow."

"Pizza it is," Gavin said, rubbing his hands together.

"Pizza sounds perfect. I'm just going to go change. When my door's fixed, I'll explain."

Gavin lifted the door easily and nodded to her. "Sounds good to me. The frame's not broken. I'll have it fixed before you get back. Devon, go get me some tools."

Sarah shut her bedroom door and sat on the bed, trying to collect her thoughts. What Tom had done truly scared the shit out of her. What in the hell was he doing, or more importantly, planning to do? Chills raced down her body as she rubbed her arms. She knew he'd been upset, but to go as far as breaking down her door was too much. It was time to call Stephen.

Picking up her house phone from the bedside table, she called Evelyn. Two rings went by until she answered. "Hey, Sarah, what's up?"

"Ev, I need you to send Stephen over."

"What's happened?" Evelyn's voice deepened at her concern.

"Tom broke down my door. Devon ran after him, but he got away."

A large intake of breath echoed over the phone. "Shit, we're on our way."

"Thanks, Ev."

Sarah hung up and walked over to her closet grabbing a pair of jeans and a T-shirt. Her hands were shaking so badly, buttoning the pants was almost impossible. All the information she was about to tell the guys would either break their building relationship or put a huge dent in it. She couldn't even begin to imagine how they would take things.

The sound of a drill made her jump. Anxiously, Sarah paced the floor trying to buy some time, but she knew she needed to get this out before Evelyn and Stephen showed up. How in the world could she tell the men who she likely would be spending the rest of her life with that for the last year she made bets on which men to sleep with?

Uncertainly, she walked out of the room. Gavin gave her a big smile until he noticed, and probably felt, her distress. He tested the door and shut it.

"All done. See, no problem. Devon!" Gavin called, looking toward the kitchen. She could see how tense he appeared. The way her body shook, she knew he could probably tell this wasn't going to be good.

Devon walked out of the kitchen, wiping his hands. "I was just getting rid of the chicken and washing the dishes. Pizza's on its way."

"I might as well tell you both before Evelyn and Stephen get here." Sarah took a deep breath and gestured for them to sit down while she paced in front of them. When they were ready, she nodded, more to jumpstart her mouth than anything.

"Tom and I met almost a year ago. It was at a club in Corpus." She paused to look at them. "Tom was one of my first bets." When they remained silent, she proceeded. "The girls and I have played the game Bets a while now. We…bet each other on who to take home. Gavin, Devon, I'm sorry, but you were both bets. That was, of course, until everyone figured out who you were," she said, looking at Devon.

"That night, Gavin, I didn't approach you the second time because of the bet. I *wanted* to be with you."

"Bets." Gavin laughed. "You girls bet on men?" He turned toward Devon. "Is it just me or does that sound more like a man's kind of game? Bets!" He laughed.

Devon threw him an angry look. "It might be funny to you, but has it occurred to you that this guy, *a bet*, is now after Sarah? That is the stupidest, most dangerous game I've ever heard of. And what about Stephen and Brandon, do they know about this game?"

Sarah looked down. "Yes, they know. We've already told them to butt out. Stephen doesn't like it at all, but Brandon's more easygoing. He thinks we're allowed to make our own decisions. Plus, they kind of watch over us and scan who we leave with. I'm not sure exactly how or what they do, but they've told us no on some of them."

"Unbelievable," Devon said aghast.

A knock at the door made Sarah's stomach twist even tighter. Gavin held up his hand when she walked forward. He went and opened the door, looking back at her for assurance.

"Are you okay?" Evelyn ran up, embracing her tightly.

"I'm fine Just a little shaken, that's all."

"Devon, it's good to see you. Sorry, I don't think we've met," Stephen said, holding out his hand to Gavin.

"Gavin. I'll be new to the pack."

"Glad to hear both of you are joining us. So what's going on here?" Stephen asked, examining the door.

Sarah noticed he wore his police uniform. He must have been on patrol. She held Evelyn's hand while they walked closer toward him.

"Tom was a bet I met at the beginning of the game. When he wanted to see me again, I declined. Let's just say he didn't take it too well. He's been prank calling me ever since, but today..." Sarah shivered. "Today he decided to knock my door in."

"Tell him about the call you received Saturday morning."

She looked at Gavin and then back to Devon. "He called, and when I acknowledged him, he said he witnessed a confrontation between the three of us outside of the Martini Bar. He had to have been watching."

"Sarah! You didn't tell me this," Evelyn squealed, tightening her hand. I would have made Stephen keep a closer eye on you."

"It's the first I've heard about it, too," Devon said, looking up at her.

"I didn't think it was a big deal." Sarah shifted her feet while she fought not to get defensive.

"It's a big deal," Stephen said, looking at her. "All right, what arrangements do you guys have going on here? I take it you're our newest threesome."

Sarah blushed while Evelyn slapped at him. "I told you not to say anything, dammit!"

"What, Evey? I have to know. It's police business."

"Sorry," Evelyn whispered.

"It's fine." Sarah let out a sigh. "I'm staying here. The guys are staying in Devon's apartment, three doors down."

"Not anymore. I want at least one of you here with her at all times. Rotate, do shifts, but I can't be on patrol twenty-four seven, plus I'll have calls to go to. I'll make a report, but unless you have a last name or something more I can go on, we're at a dead end."

"I know the license plate number. I memorized it."

Stephen nodded for Devon to follow him outside while Gavin walked to stand next to her and Evelyn. "Devon can stay tonight. I'll stay tomorrow. Is that all right with you?"

Sarah looked up to meet his gaze. "Yeah, that's fine, but what about you? What are you going to do?"

He winked at her and smiled at Evelyn. "I'll keep a look out. Plus, I'll have first dibs if he comes again. Oh, and I'm glad it's Devon tonight. I have to meet Trevor at the fire station in Corpus early in the morning. I wouldn't want to wake you. I might be a little late on getting back though. He mentioned something about wanting to talk to me about the details of the wedding. I think it's being delayed."

"Oh. So you're a firefighter?"

"Yes. Most of us werewolves are in a similar occupation, cops, firefighters, paramedics, even military. Our blood is wired to protect, so to speak."

"Wow, I didn't know that."

Sarah looked to Evelyn raising her eyebrows. "Stephen, Ayden, Trevor, now Gavin... What in the world does Brandon do?"

"He plays stocks. Pretty damn good at it if I do say so myself. Of course Stephen thinks he needs to get a job away from the house. What about Devon? What does he do?"

Sarah looked at Evelyn at a loss of what to say. She had no idea. Quickly, she turned to Gavin, but he just shrugged.

"Doctor," Devon said, walking in with Stephen.

Sarah's mouth dropped to the floor. "Doctor? You went to college after you left?"

A knife stabbed into her heart. It took her over a year to rip herself out of depression so she could attend night courses. Even that turned out to be a chore. She pined for him, waited for him so they could go together. But he left and just picked up his life like nothing major or traumatic happened. How was that possible?

"Not immediately, no. I started college when I was twenty-two. After stitching up repeated pack members trying to challenge me, it was either a doctor or a vet. I chose doctor."

His confession still hurt. So maybe it took him longer than it did her, but she still couldn't believe it. When he was younger he'd always talked about becoming a mechanic. She liked that idea. He was forever working on his motorcycle. Sarah started to realize how much they both changed.

Stephen cleared his throat, pulling her from her thoughts. Sarah looked up. "Oh right. You take care, Evelyn. Call me tomorrow. We'll go over the plans for movie night."

She hugged Sarah tightly. "I look forward to it. Nicole can't wait to meet you. Officially, that is. We're all going to be great friends. You'll see."

"I'm sure we will be." The weight of the events had really started to take their toll. Sarah could feel her legs growing heavier by the second.

Stephen wrapped his arm through Evelyn's and opened the door. "I'll patrol extra tonight and run these numbers to see what we come up with. You'll be getting a call, Devon. Welcome to the family, guys."

The pizza guy jumped in surprise, his hand midair. "I'll take care of that," Devon said, walking her friends outside. Turning to Gavin, Sarah threw herself into his arms. She felt so mentally exhausted and the need to feel comforted made it hard to resist the pull.

"You're tired." His hand wrapped around the base of her neck, and he rested his cheek on the top of her head. Having him close made her feel so safe. She almost wished he wouldn't be leaving tonight.

"Yeah, it's been a long day. I missed you."

The door opened behind them, but she didn't move. "I missed you, too." He quickly leaned down and kissed her forehead.

"Gavin, why don't you sit down with Sarah so I can make everyone's plates?"

She turned to look at Devon, surprised. While she was led to the couch, she could feel her muscles tense with every step. Her attention went back to Devon. The fact that he let Gavin tend to her was the last thing she would have expected. Were they making progress so soon? She really hoped so.

Chapter 11

After five minutes of arguing, she finally gave in and laid her head in Gavin's lap while her feet where in Devon's. It didn't take long before the feeling of her hair being played with and her feet being touched nearly rendered her unconscious.

A soft brush of lips across Sarah's fingertips hardly registered. The sound of the nightly news faded in the background while she closed her eyes and focused on the calming sensations she felt from Devon messaging her feet.

"Sarah, I'm going to go. I'll see you tomorrow when you get home from work."

"Hmm, okay." Suddenly realizing what Gavin had said, she bolted upright. He was leaving, which meant she'd be alone with Devon. "Wait. Are you sure? What happens if you see Tom? You'll be alone."

"I'll be fine. If it makes you feel better, I'll call for Devon if anything happens."

Sarah sat up, looking at him seriously. "You promise?"

Gavin laughed and kissed her gently on the lips. "All you have to do is ask. I'd never lie to you."

"All right. Be careful, please."

"Of course. I wouldn't dare give Devon the satisfaction of having you all to himself. I'll see you tomorrow."

"Okay."

Sarah watched the two guys nod to each other. She wasn't sure how she knew, but somehow they had just communicated without actually saying anything. The sound of the door closing caused her heart to race. Could she do this, really be alone for the first time in years with Devon?

"If you're tired, we can go lay in the bed. I'll put you to sleep. You don't have to worry about anything else. I promise not to touch you if don't want me to do."

A little too quickly, Sarah shook her head. *Smooth Sarah. If you didn't look scared before, you sure did just then.*

Standing and walking to the room, she could hear him following behind her. Her body tightened, causing her nipples to harden painfully. Whether she'd made the decision about being with Devon or not, it seemed her body had already decided for her.

"Devon." Sarah turned around, looking at him. Fear of the unknown made her heart race even faster.

"What's wrong? Tell me." The soothing tone of his voice settled though her.

She didn't say a word. Grabbing his hand, she put it over her heart. The way he looked down at her caused tears to come to her eyes. So much pain existed between them. Was there a chance they could end it here, tonight?

Devon's arms wrapped around her, pulling her body into his. For minutes he held her, stoking the back of her hair. Sarah cried about everything she could think of, letting the pain finally release. When hiccups rocked her body, Devon lifted her face.

"I hurt you badly, and for that, I'll forever be sorry. But trust me when I tell you this, I'll never hurt or leave you again. I promise. Nothing will take me away from you now. I've made sure of that."

Devon's lips eased against hers. She didn't think. Sarah pressed desperately more into him. Problems would be there for them to face, but right now, she wanted to experience what she'd missed all these years. The need to taste, to drink in every ounce of him she could manage wrenched at her very soul.

"Sarah, I missed you."

Wetness slid across her cheek, and it took her a moment to realize the tears didn't come from her. Devon kissed her passionately, clutching her back. Just the familiar feel of his touch came rushing back.

Holding him as tightly as she could, she pressed herself as close as she could get, still feeling too far apart. Devon's hands quickly lifted her by her thighs. Straddling his waist, she let him pull off her shirt while she untucked his.

"Don't ever leave me again. Ever."

"Never," he whispered against her lips.

Sarah felt the bed under her back as Devon lowered her. She kicked off the rest of her clothes only to realize he beat her at removing his own. The awe at watching his muscles flex while he lowered himself had wetness seeping from her pussy. This wasn't the same Devon she remembered. Not even close.

Starting off at her neck, he kissed his way down to her breasts. In slow torturing circles, he teased her nipple, pulling it with his teeth at the end, only to move on to the next one. Sarah moaned, arching her back with the impatience to have his weight on her.

While his hands pushed her thighs wide, she tried to control her breathing. The intensity at which she wanted this to happen scared the controlling part of her mind, but she was willing to let go of everything if it meant regaining what she lost so long ago.

* * * *

So many times Devon dreamed of this exact scenario happening, but never once did it feel this real. Sarah's scent, her essence, pulled at everything that resided inside. Finally, he'd have her, even if he'd prefer different terms. Gavin was something he'd have to become accustomed to, but if it meant having Sarah, then he was almost positive he could do it.

Trailing his lips down the valley between her breasts, Devon inhaled deeply. She smelled exactly the way he remembered, lavender with the slight mix of jasmine, a smell he tried to duplicate a million times and never succeeded.

The farther down he got, the stronger the pull became. The need to bury his face on her inner thigh and mark her taunted his mind. He wanted to, God how he wanted to sink his teeth into her, but it was immoral. After making Gavin agree not to, he couldn't turn around and do it. It was something they'd have to do together.

Hovering above the wetness of Sarah's pussy, Devon took a deep breath and lowered himself. Slowly, he trailed his fingers along her folds, feeling her shake beneath him. The sweetness of her taste swept across his senses, igniting an inferno of need, a need to touch, to taste, a need to take in as much of her as he possibly could.

Sliding his tongue inside of her opening, he felt her arch to receive him deeper. Repeatedly, he thrust, taking in as much of her juices as he could. He traced the inside of her pussy, feeling her grip around him tighter and tighter.

Impatient to taste her cum, Devon sucked on her clit and eased a finger into her slowly. Sarah bucked wildly as her orgasm rocked her body. Her scent hit him in waves. Tears came to his eyes as he fought the wolf inside of him. All he could hear was the screaming inside of his head begging him to forever make her his. Never had the pull been this powerful.

* * * *

Stars danced in front of Sarah's eyes as she fought to focus her vision. She could feel Devon moving back up her body. The path of heat he left in his wake made her ready to come all over again. The feel of hard, smooth skin caressed her body as he slid against her. An urge to trace her tongue down every inch of his cock was almost uncontrollable, but the need to have him fill her overpowered everything.

"Devon, make love to me. I need to feel you inside of me, please."

He didn't hesitate, didn't ask questions. The width of his cock stretched her while he eased his length into of her opening. Digging her nails into his back, she moaned at the overall sensation of her pussy gripping his thickness. Every inch he surged deeper sparked new currents of pleasure to burst through her body.

"This feel so right, so…" Sarah moaned.

"Perfect," Devon said, finishing for her.

"Yes. I've always thought we fit perfectly together."

Devon's tongue slid against hers as she felt him plunge the rest of his length inside of her. She moaned into his mouth, wrapping her legs around his waist. His rough hand grasped her hip while he began to thrust leisurely, reaching impossibly deeper and deeper with each push.

The friction against Sarah's clit made her cling to his neck even tighter. Their bodies connected at every space imaginable, and she wasn't going to give an inch of room for them to be apart.

She suddenly realized how consumed she felt by him. Every part of her mind begged to have Devon claim her in some way, and it had nothing to do with sex. . While her thoughts raced with ways to never be separated from him again, she completely lost the connection to her body. The orgasm that blindsided her had her screaming out Devon's name.

His cock plunged harder, making her release back to back until finally she felt his warmth explode inside of her. The spell she was under suddenly broke, and reality crashed before her in a blinding wave of dizziness. She looked up at Devon just as shocked as he looked back at her, but neither of them said a word. Sarah couldn't, wouldn't even broach the fact that they'd just had unprotected sex. To do that would open a wound she wasn't ready to face.

Chapter 12

The heat surrounding Sarah caused her to stir from sleep. The sun was just beginning to rise, casting light in through the curtains. She opened her eyes groggily to see Devon staring down at her, smiling. Wrapping her arms around his waist, she snuggled closer against his body.

After their shower, she'd fallen right to sleep. There was no telling how long she'd been out, but she felt completely revived and ready to have him inside of her again. The thought of what happened before scared her, but now that she'd slept on the idea, what occurred seemed to feel right, almost fated. She decided for once not to worry about the future and to take one day at a time.

Trailing her fingers down his stomach, she came to rest at the base of his cock. She wrapped her hand along the width, slowly stroking up, feeling him become harder at her touch. He looked at her uneasily but didn't say anything as she continued to caress him.

"Devon, I want you to make love to me again. Whatever happens happens. No blame. We'll never speak of it if you don't want to."

"Are you sure this is what you want?"

No thinking. You want this. Don't deny it or overanalyze it, Sarah! Just say yes. "Yes." *There that wasn't so hard.*

Devon's arms embraced her against his body while his lips went to her throat. She was pulled on top of him and didn't waste any time sliding his cock into her wet pussy. Easing down slowly, she felt him fill her until there was nowhere else for him to possibly go.

"Fuck, Sarah. You can't imagine how good you feel. You're so wet and tight. I don't ever want this to end."

"Me either. I missed you being inside of me."

"You missed what being inside of you? Say, it for me, baby. Tell me what you missed."

"Your cock. You."

He moaned while she rotated her hips. Sarah pushed against his chest as she began to take his length into her faster. Catching their reflection in the dresser mirror, she watched her breasts bounce as she moved up and down. She saw Devon look over, and she watched him study their bodies.

Easily, he lifted her off him and placed her on her knees, facing the direction of the mirror. She watched in awe as he pressed his wide chest against her back.

"I want you to watch and remember the way we look together. I want you to see the pleasure we put on each other's faces. Know that this is what it looks like to truly make love to someone. It's more than sex, Sarah. What we share is so unlike what you've shared with others. No one can replace the bond between you and me. Gavin may in his own way, but what you both share will be completely different than what we share. Watch the way you react to my touch."

Sarah observed Devon's hand trail across her stomach and inch its way toward her breast. She shivered underneath his touch. A moan broke through her throat as his finger entered her pussy from behind, completely surprising her. She wanted to lean forward, but he held her up so she could see.

As he explored her depths, he brushed his fingertips across the hardness of her nipple. Sarah watched her lips part while she breathed heavily against the pleasure. Her cheeks blossomed into a light pink as his finger increased in rhythm. Focusing on herself proved to be impossible when she could hardly keep her eyes open.

"You see how my touch affects you? That's love, Sarah. Besides Gavin, has anyone else ever made you feel close to what you're feeling now? And be truthful."

"Never," Sarah whispered. And he was right. No one, in all the years he'd been gone, had brought her to the brink of ecstasy but the two of them.

"And no one ever will. That's the beauty of the bond. This, and our love for each other will never get old, will never die. You'll never tire of my touch or my presence. We might argue, but we'll never truly feel hate for each other. Mates, soul mates, life partners, we're all that and more. Nothing can tear us apart, not even ourselves because, as impossible as it seems, our love is woven so deep it's impenetrable."

Devon cupped her breast and allowed her to lean forward. His cock filled her from behind until all that existed were the two of them in that moment. Lifting her face, he made her watch as he brought her body to the heights of passion.

Seeing his muscles flex behind her while he slid his cock to new depths brought her over the edge repeatedly. She could feel her pussy contracting around him. Pulling her back completely against his chest, Sarah felt Devon's finger slide over her clit. Bright lights flashed before her eyes and heat filled her at the same time. As he shot his cum deep inside of her, she didn't have one regret what transpired between them.

They both collapsed to the bed, panting. Sarah rolled over to stare into Devon's face. He rested with his eyes closed, a look a pure delight on his face. The outside of his lips were turned up into a smile. He was beautiful.

"Everything's going to be okay, right?"

His eyes opened, and he turned his head in her direction. The smile he wore turned tender. "Everything's going to be great. I'll make you happy. I know Gavin will. He adores you. We have each other now. That's all that matters. Anything else is trivial."

Sarah kissed his lips and stood from the bed. "I'm getting in the shower. I've got to be in the office today."

Devon lifted to a sitting position. His face creased with worry. "Will you do something for me?"

"Sure." She walked over, sitting back down on the edge of the bed.

"Can you take my phone today? I want to keep yours in case that guy calls back. I'm going to get together with Stephen and see if he's learned anything."

"All right. You'll call me when you know something, right?"

"Yes, of course."

Sarah nodded and walked to the shower. The last thing she wanted to do was go into work today, but Devon and Gavin still needed time alone. Even though her ex made a remarkable turnaround in the last twenty-four hours, would it last after she left? She'd find out soon enough.

* * * *

Gavin left the firehouse in better spirits than he arrived in. Trevor happened to be a great guy and things were already set up when he arrived. But being away from Sarah drove him almost to the point of insanity. He couldn't help but wonder what had happened between her and Devon last night. Did things go well, or did the domineering cowboy complicate things worse than they already were?

Having to share Sarah wasn't something Gavin liked, but he wasn't stupid enough to make her choose. As a recently divorced father of a five-year-old daughter, he'd already been in the exact spot before. Ultimately, he wasn't the one chosen. Although, he hadn't marked his ex-wife, he did love her.

Much like Devon and Sarah, Hilary and he had gone to school together. They had only been married for three years when Gavin contracted lycanthropy. He'd been so focused on why Hilary had been acting strange that when their fire truck approached the intersection at the high rate of speed, he hadn't even noticed the white Honda

Accord until the second before it plowed into them. One minute he was sitting there in the back seat, and the next he was getting slammed into his buddy. Everything turned into slow motion as he felt himself falling toward the passenger's side. The road came into view through the window and he could see himself getting closer to the asphalt.

Gavin felt weightless, yet heavy as he fought against gravity. The feeling didn't last long because his memory blanked after that. The crew said he'd hit his head on the roof of the truck, and at some point he probably did, but he couldn't remember it. All he knew was what he'd been told. He suffered a major concussion, a broken arm, and a few lacerations.

When the first full moon rolled around, he found out he'd caught more than a mini vacation from the outcome of that accident. How exactly, he wasn't sure. They had to have been all bleeding, and all thrown together when the truck finally came to a stop. Whoever he'd caught it from never said a thing, and they sure as hell didn't show up at the pack he had discovered on his own. For months he waited, but to no avail, he was left to face his new life as a werewolf alone.

Gavin thought back to the day when he told Hilary about what he was. At first she thought he was losing his mind. She even made calls to try to get him committed, but ultimately he had to show her firsthand. He'd thought his wife could handle the change. She couldn't. The mere thought of her being with someone not human repulsed her, and soon, she began seeing another man.

Gavin tried to make her love him again, but he ultimately knew their divorce was probably for the best. A deep need to find a mate pulled at him. When he received the invitation for the wedding, he knew he needed to go, no matter what.

The moment he saw Sarah everything clicked, and like a punch in the gut, he knew that no one would ever hold his heart like she would. Her history, her past, nothing mattered but being together and making a future with each other, whatever future she chose.

Devon constantly brought out his defenses, but he couldn't deny the love Sarah carried for the cowboy. From experience, he knew he couldn't change her mind. He'd like to think he learned from his past. Of course, having to deal with *this* other man was something completely different than what he'd ever been through before.

Pulling into the apartment complex, Gavin noticed Devon standing outside of Sarah's apartment with Stephen. He quickly got out, walking to meet the men. Curiosity about new information made him move faster.

"Gavin, how was the interview?" Stephen asked, shaking his hand.

"Good, I start next Monday. So, did you learn anything from the license plate?"

Devon and Stephen looked over at each other, not saying anything, but Gavin could feel their disappointment. Confused, he lifted his hands gesturing for them to start talking.

"The car was reported stolen out of Corpus Christi two weeks ago. It seems we're at a dead end."

"You're fucking kidding me." He ran his hand through his hair. Who in the hell was this guy? Even a random stalker wouldn't steal a car.

"I'm afraid not. Both of you might want to keep a close eye on Sarah. I know if it were Evelyn, she wouldn't be leaving my side. I don't care if I had to go to work with her. This guy is bad news, and I don't like the fact that he knows who Sarah's friends are. That puts all the girls in danger until he's caught."

"So what do we do?" Gavin asked.

"I think I'll let Ayden know. He can send some of the pack to watch over the other girls without them knowing. As long as you both protect Sarah, then everything should be fine. Evelyn would kill me if I didn't make sure I did everything possible to keep her friend safe."

"She'll be with one of us at all times," Devon assured him.

"Good, well, I'm headed back to the house. I have Brandon keeping Evelyn occupied so she won't go into work today. We can't afford for anything to happen to her."

"Why is that?"

Stephen looked at Gavin and smiled proudly. "Because I'm going to be a father. Evelyn doesn't want anyone to know yet, but it won't be long before she spills to all her friends. I, of course, already knew from her scent, but Brandon and I kept silent until she found out for herself. We have a doctor's appointment next Monday. We can't wait. I'm surprised you both didn't pick up the scent when she was here."

"I did," Devon said in a low voice.

The pure panic pouring off of him made Gavin take a step back. He wasn't quite sure what to make out of the anxiety racing through the cowboy. Shouldn't he be upset or hurt because of their loss? Why scared? It made no sense.

"Congratulations," they both said at the same time, in two separate tones.

Stephen smiled. "Thanks, but please don't tell Sarah. I want Evelyn to surprise her with the news."

"You're secret is safe with us," Devon said.

Gavin threw his hand up in a wave as Stephen said his goodbyes. Something felt off, and the quicker he straightened out things with Devon, the soon he could get the guy to drop him off at Sarah's office. The need to be with her, to make sure she was all right nearly caused him to get in his car and drive straight over there. Problem was he didn't have a clue as to where she worked. He could sniff her out or use the pull, but it would take too long.

Devon headed in the direction of Sarah's apartment. Gavin followed, closing the door behind him. He didn't even wait for the cowboy to turn around before he lost patience.

"So what happened last night? You didn't get kicked out so it must not have gone too bad."

A smile lit his face, and the expression of happiness and love turned Gavin's stomach, but a part of him calmed at knowing maybe they were all one step closer to being at a more likeable stage.

"It was wonderful. I haven't been this happy or complete since before I left."

"Well, that's good, but truthfully I don't care how you feel. I want to know how Sarah is. Is she happy with the way things are going?"

Devon glared at him. "She's more than happy, I think."

"You think? What do you mean, you think? Either she is or she isn't. The question's not really that hard to answer."

"Well, when she left she looked happy. Hell, she was glowing."

"But…you're not telling me something. I can feel it. What have you done?"

Devon looked at the carpet and so many different emotions hit him that Gavin closed his eyes to decipher them.

"You're scared about something."

"Come on, Gavin. There's a man after Sarah. What, I can't be scared?"

Gavin burst out laughing. "No, you're not scared about that. When you just said it, you reeked of confidence. You believe you can protect her. What are you afraid of?"

Devon advanced so quickly Gavin barely side-stepped. The anger clouding the room could have choked him.

"What did you do?"

"You stay out of my business. Do you hear me?"

It was his turn to get angry. He could feel heat flare through his body and seep from his skin. "Sarah is my business, and you better start remembering that! If you've done something, then I need to know. What part of 'she's my mate, too,' do you not understand?"

The tension melted off of Devon. Gavin could see it in the way his body hunched down. Devon was silent as he walked to the sofa and slowly sat down.

"We...Sarah and I didn't use protection last night. I'm not sure what scares me more, the risk of pregnancy itself, or her emotional state if she does end up..."

At a loss for words or even thoughts, Gavin walked up to the other side of the couch and sat down. He never even considered thinking this far ahead so soon.

"After everything in your past, you didn't think to wear protection?" Gavin said it softly, so not to offend him. The question was genuine.

Devon looked at him and held his gaze. "This isn't an excuse, but neither of us could control ourselves the first time. I couldn't even think clearly. The pull grabbed a hold of me so strong that all of my attention stayed focused on not betraying you and marking her. The second time, this morning, she told me, *what happens, happens*."

"Thank you, for not marking her. I would have been offended. I truly appreciate you not going behind my back. So, do you think it's possible maybe Sarah wants a child?"

"I'm not sure, maybe." Devon rubbed his eyes. "I'll give her what she wants, but that doesn't mean it won't scare the shit out of me. If anything were to happen this time..."

"Listen, let's not worry about the what-ifs until a few more weeks. We'll know before anyone, even her."

"You're not angry? She is your mate too."

"Angry, no. If Sarah does end up being pregnant by you, it's still part of her. I have a daughter. Did you know that?"

Devon looked at him shocked. "No, you never mentioned it to me. How old is she?"

Gavin pulled a picture out of his wallet. "Annabelle is five. She lives with her mother and her new stepfather."

"She's beautiful. The blonde curls remind me of Sarah. Is she..."

"Werewolf? No." Gavin shook his head "I contracted the disease shortly after she was born. My wife couldn't handle what I turned into, and I believe she'd already met Dave then so one thing turned into another, and we eventually ended up getting divorced."

"I'm sorry."

Gavin slid the picture back in his wallet. "Don't be. I get to see my daughter when I choose. My wife isn't that ruthless. Plus, I have Sarah."

Devon nodded, agreeing. Not wanting to waste any time, Gavin stood. "I need you to drop me off at her office. Someone needs to be there, and since I haven't really gotten to see her, I would like to be the one."

"Of course, but do you really think she's going to want someone tagging along while she's trying to do her job?"

Gavin raised his eyebrow. "I don't think she really has an option. It's that, or I'm throwing her over my shoulder and bringing her home. There's no way I'm risking anyone catching her alone."

"I like the way you think." Devon smiled at him and grabbed his keys. "So, where are we going?"

Gavin's eyes widened. "I don't know. I thought you'd have a better idea where her office was considering this is where you're from. I guess I can call her."

"I have her phone, and she has mine. I'll look through her numbers and maybe call Evelyn or Stephen. They'll give us the address."

Gavin followed Devon outside and got into his truck. The sound of the loud diesel felt oddly fitting for a place like this. He looked around at the palm trees and the sea gulls flying in the gray sky. He never felt more at home. Now, once they found Sarah, he'd feel even better.

Chapter 13

If Sarah played one more game of Bejeweled Blitz, she'd scream. Looking at her watch, she grabbed her purse, ready to meet her friends for their daily lunch ritual. Evelyn hadn't come into work today, and Melissa was out showing a house, so she called explaining she might be a little late. Julie and Natalie were already on their way.

"If I have any calls, just take a message. I don't have my phone on me today," Sarah said, stopping at the receptionist's desk.

"Will do, honey."

The older woman smiled as Sarah grabbed a peppermint out of the woven basket on the counter and waved goodbye. Stunned, Sarah stopped and stared. Devon and Gavin leaned against the truck, both looking good enough to eat. She smiled at the warmth crossing their faces and walked to meet them.

The heels of her stilettos clicked against the sidewalk as she slowed her pace. It wouldn't look too good if she acted as excited as she felt.

"What are you both doing here? I thought you'd be off doing… guy things." What exactly they'd be doing she couldn't imagine, but her guess consisted of them being together. She needed the bonding to happen quickly. Every minute without feeling their presence ate away at her until she felt the compulsion to rush home to see them.

"Well, Stephen stopped by." Devon didn't say anymore. She noticed how he studied her face.

"And? What did he say?"

"We're at a dead end. The car didn't reveal anything."

"Oh, so what does that mean?"

The guys looked at each other and then looked back at her. "I'm going to spend the rest of the day with you until you've finished work."

"Oh no you're not," Sarah laughed, shaking her head no.

Gavin's eyes narrowed, but the smile remained."Yes...I am. With Tom still on the loose, I'm not risking leaving you alone. Either I can stay with you at the office or you can call an early day, but it's your choice."

Sarah turned to Devon, who raised his hands in surrender. "You're kidding me, right? You can't be serious."

"I'm dead serious."

Gavin walked over, dropping his head. "Sarah, please don't make this harder than it has to be. I want to keep you safe. Please allow me to do that. If something happened to you, Devon and I would never forgive ourselves."

Placing her hands on her hips, she tilted her head, maintaining eye contact. "Is this just for today, or are we talking about tomorrow and the next day and the day after that?"

"For as long as it takes," Devon said, coming up beside them. "Sarah, I'm not going to pretend you're not pissed right now. I know the temper you keep hidden, but do us a favor and think about this. There's a man who's after you. He knows where you live and probably where you work. He's seen your car, and more than likely, he's waiting to make his next move. You possibly might not be the only target. If he saw you with your friends, they're at risk, too. Why do you think Stephen kept Evelyn home today?"

Shaken, Sarah let the words sink in. It was one thing to assume everything would be fine, but the situation changed when she thought her friends might be at risk.

"All right," she whispered. "Fine, you both can take turns coming to work with me, but right now, I'm headed to lunch with the girls. I'm assuming that means Gavin's coming with me so why don't you follow us, and we'll all have lunch together? You can get to know my friends. They're a big part of my life, so I guess you've just inherited them, too."

"Let's go. I'll follow you."

Sarah walked to her car with Gavin following. When he didn't insist on driving she was thankful. She got in and headed toward the beach restaurant where everyone surely would be waiting. The ride was quiet as she mulled over her thoughts. In just days, they'd all been thrown into this whirlwind of a situation, and she wasn't sure how to take things. Everything, from the events of her sexual experiences with the men to Tom floated around her mind, taunting her emotions.

Pulling into the parking lot, Sarah sat quietly in the seat. She could do this. Introducing them to her friends was the easy part. The following minutes were the ones that would matter. They'd either embrace her choice, or they wouldn't. Either way, it wasn't as if she could go back. The thought only made her heart accelerate even more. This situation was as permanent as it got, and she couldn't control anything about it.

Movement from the corner of her eye made her turn toward Gavin. The fingers he brushed against her cheek sent an odd, calming sensation through her. "You worry too much. I'm here for you if you ever want to talk."

She smiled and grabbed his hand, kissing his knuckles. "Thank you. You make me feel better. I'm just worried about how things are going to go. Everything's happening so fast. I understand, but they won't. They'll have no idea why, in just days, I've gone from *not needing a man* to needing two."

"If they're you're true friends, they'll accept whatever you decide to tell them."

"Evelyn has, but Melissa, Julie, and Natalie, I just don't know."

Devon tapped on the glass, a look of confusion on his face. She could tell he was tired. Knowing him, he probably still hadn't slept.

"They will, trust me. And if they don't, then maybe they weren't your true friends. Friendship holds no judgment."

"I'm not sure I agree one hundred percent, but I guess we'll see. Let's go eat, shall we? Devon needs to head back soon and get some rest."

"Sarah, I know you don't like the position you've been put in with us having to go to work with you, but would you consider taking a small vacation? At least until this guy is caught."

Opening the door, Sarah got out of the car and looked over the short roof at Gavin. "How long is this supposed to take? It's possible we may never see Tom again. I'd be taking off of work for nothing. I can't afford to miss potential sales, and I don't like having to put my clients off either."

"All right. If this is what you want to do, forget I mentioned it."

Conflicted, Sarah walked into the restaurant. The loud laughter coming from their usual table died the moment they noticed the two men following behind her.

"Well, well, look who we have here," Melissa said, glaring.

Sarah immediately remembered their confrontation at the bar. "Knock it off, Mel, not today, okay."

"Have you lost your freaking mind? Am I the only one who remembers the weeks, shit, months of your pain?"

"Try years, and no, I haven't forgotten. I've learned to forgive and so should you."

Devon and Gavin pulled up a chair, sitting on each side of her. The girls stared, confused. Sarah rolled her eyes as she began to relay the news of Tom to them.

"So, you're telling me that hot ass guy you left with almost a year ago has turned all stalker on you?" Julie asked, shocked. "Fucking amazing. I knew he seemed a little off, but wow."

"Who made that bet for you anyway?"

She looked at Melissa, raising her eyebrow. "You did, genius."

"Well, shit, Sarah. I don't remember anymore. We play this game every weekend. How am I supposed to remember some guy you left with a year ago? I mean, seriously, I try my best to forget their names."

"Melissa, you may not remember him, but I'm sure he remembers all of you. I want everyone to be careful until this guy is caught. He shouldn't be hard to miss. His eyes will give him away."

"Eyes," Julie whispered. "That's right! His eyes were the lightest blue I've ever seen."

"Holy shit! I know who you're talking about now. Dark hair, light eyes, a little over six foot, kind of on the lean side, but still pretty built. Wow, I was so proud of that bet. Too bad he turned out to be a fruit."

"Yeah, well, that fruit could be after any of us so I want everyone on the lookout for him. If you see him, call Stephen or me. Devon and Gavin will be with me at all times."

"Speaking of which, what is going on with you three? Please don't tell me I'm seeing another Evelyn romance in the making."

Sarah looked at the redhead and tried to control her anger. "And if you are, then what, Melissa?"

"Then nothing, but how? I feel like I'm missing something. You've known these guys for what, five minutes? Now they're your entourage? Why not stay with me or Ev? Why risk this," she said, gesturing her hand toward Devon, "again? He hurt you," she whispered, her pain showing on her face.

"Melissa." Sarah fought the tears in her eyes. "You have to know I loved him. I still do. Love like that never truly dies."

She grew quiet so long the food arrived. Sarah was surprised Devon, most of all, remained quiet throughout their conversation. He usually stood up to people who spoke their minds so easily. The fact that he didn't start an argument with her friend gave him mega bonus points in her book.

"So, tell me something. If you love Devon, why are you not denying Hotness over there? You're basically admitting to wanting to be with both of them. How are all of you okay with that? Guys don't submit so easily. Dammit! Sarah, you're hiding something," Melissa snapped, frustrated. "This shit just doesn't happen? Men don't agree to relationships like this."

"Now is not the time to discuss this," Gavin said softly.

Sarah picked at her food as throbbing in her head nearly made her sick. Maybe taking off the rest of the day wasn't such a bad idea. She kept quiet while she tried forcing something in her stomach. Melissa's attitude toward Devon really upset her. More than anyone, she knew the pain he caused her, and yes, her friend's intentions were good, but shit, the decision was hers to make and no one else's.

Gavin rested his hand on her thigh and peace spiked with a sense of heat filled her. "Devon, do you have my phone on you?"

She watched while he pulled it out of his pocket. "Thanks." Sarah hit the office's number and waited until the reception answered. "Hey, this is Sarah. Listen, I'm not feeling so well. My head is killing me. I'll be going home. Can you just take a message for anyone who calls and tell them I'll get in touch with them tomorrow? Thanks."

Gavin's fingers tightened on her thigh, and she looked up to see a grin spread across his face. Placing the phone in her purse, Sarah handed Devon's back to him. "Well, ladies, I'm going home."

The smile that came to Sarah's face felt plastered on. Damn, she really had wanted this meeting to go better. The men instantly stood beside her. She placed money on the table and took both of their hands. "Let's go home, shall we?"

"Gladly," Devon said, kissing her forehead.

"You all have a great day."

Melissa quickly stood. "Sarah, wait. Devon, I'm sorry. But you know Sarah is like my sister. I hated seeing her go through pain. If she forgives you, then I'll try my best. I trust her judgment, but I know you all are hiding something. One thing before you leave…if you hurt her again, I'll hunt you down myself."

Devon laughed. "Thanks, Melissa, but I'm not going anywhere ever again. I love her. Always have and always will."

"Me too," Melissa said, hugging her. "I love you, Sarah. You know that. Go get some rest. You look paler than usual. I think this mess is taking its toll on you."

"I love you, too, Mel. Call me later."

Leaving the restaurant, Sarah couldn't remember feeling more relieved for instant peace and quiet. The need to lie back and relax sounded so good she could feel the tension leaving her body. Devon stopped, wrestling in his tight pockets while they continued forward.

"Want me to drive?"

Gladly, she handed her keys to Gavin, but as she approached the car, fear nearly suffocated her. Twice, she looked around, hoping she wasn't looking at the right vehicle.

"What the…" Gavin pulled her close. "Devon!"

The sound of footsteps coming up behind them was followed by a string of curses. "I can't believe this shit. He was here, and we missed him." Devon sniffed the air, closing his eyes. "He's been gone for a few minutes."

Sarah pulled out her phone and called Stephen. It wasn't moments later she saw him fly up in his police cruiser. The damage to her car looked like a wrecking ball slammed into the side of it. Her whole driver's side door looked unrecognizable. The glass in all of her windows littered the asphalt parking lot.

"Well, this doesn't look good," Stephen said, studying the car while he walked toward them. "I hope you have insurance."

"Yeah," Sarah breathed out. "But why is he doing this? I didn't want to see him again, so what? I don't understand why rejection would cause him to react this way. None of this makes sense to me. There has to be something I'm missing."

"Stephen, is it just me, or should we be talking to Brandon? No human did this without being caught. His scent held something. It could be vampire, but the trouble with that is vampires all have different scents so it's hard to tell. I do know he's definitely not a wolf, though. I'd have picked up on that when he busted the door down."

"Well, I've only met one vampire before Brandon, and they smelled nothing alike so you could be right."

Sarah breathed heavily. "You say vampire. If he was a vampire, wouldn't I remember? I mean, I don't really know the similarities between what happens in the myths compared to reality, but I would think he would have tried to drink my blood, and I sure as hell wouldn't have forgotten that."

Stephen narrowed his eyes at her. "Tell me this, Sarah. What *do* you remember from that night?"

"Well, I'm sure as hell not going to go into detail," she said, looking at the guys uneasily. After they all remained quiet waiting for her to go on, she rolled her eyes and continued. "We left the bar and headed to a motel a few blocks away. We fucked and…" Sarah saw the images in her head so vividly she could feel her breathing slow. Calling him an amazing lover would have been an understatement, which suddenly shocked her. She'd never really thought about what happened that night.

Tom lay on top of her, the back of his hand running down her cheek to her throat. She knew they just got done having sex, but pieces of it seemed to be missing. Sarah could feel her breasts pressed against his chest while he eased her face to the side. In her trance-like state, she could feel tender kisses trailing down her jaw line, and suddenly she was at home, in her own bed.

"Oh God," Sarah whispered.

"What is it? You remember something?" Devon took a step forward, toward her and Gavin.

"It's not what I remember, it's what I can't remember. I don't know how I made it home. Did I pass out? With the game, for so long, I've tried to forget my bets. My mind didn't want to remember them. They filled the loneliness, so I didn't want to reflect on what happened behind those closed doors. But this is what he wanted me to do. He wanted me to remember…"

"You felt him as if you were there with him all over again."

Sarah looked at Gavin. "Yes." She shuddered. "It felt so real. It's hard to explain in words."

Stephen's fingers pulled at the uniform's collar as he appeared to be going over things in his mind. "If he knew you enjoyed it, he'd think you'd want to be with him again. He's probably waited so long because he figured at some point you'd come around. Now that you have two men in your life, I guess he's getting desperate. Vampires always think they have all the time in the world. This one must be starting to panic."

Stephen radioed in a tow truck and rubbed his eyes tiredly. "So, we are dealing with a vampire. Brandon and I know all about wiping memories. We did Evelyn's when I tried to remove my mark from her. Well, I hate to say this, Sarah, but I think we're going to have to let Brandon unlock whatever Tom made you forget. It's the only way we're going to know anything. But for Brandon to do this, you're going to have to let him bite you."

Sarah immediately grabbed her neck. "Does it hurt?"

Stephen laughed. "Not even close. You'll like it."

"I'm not so sure about this. What about you, Gavin? Do you feel comfortable letting her get bit?"

"Hell no, but if it helps, what do we have to lose? I want this guy off the streets."

"She's going to need one of you, or both, whatever, to be there with her when he does the bite. I don't think Evelyn's going to want her attacking Brandon. But do me a favor and mark her. This vampire's not going to get the picture until you do. Now go home and get that over with while I take care of this here. Brandon, Evelyn, and I will be over first thing in the morning."

Devon wrapped his arm around her shoulder as shouts behind them erupted in a flurry of panicked curses.

"Sarah, what the hell happened to your car!" Julie ran up, her eyes wide with fear. Melissa and Natalie followed right behind her.

"Tom happened. Now, I'm going home. You all be careful and remember, if you see him, call Evelyn so she can tell Stephen."

They all nodded, silent from the shock. Sarah wrapped her arms around Devon while he led her to the passenger side of his truck. Climbing in the middle, she waited while Gavin got in the passenger seat, and Devon started the engine.

"I think it's too soon to mark her," Gavin said, looking out of the window.

"Why is that? We're all bound together. The pull's not going to lessen. We all might as well get it over with."

"You're saying that, but do you know what that entails? Think about it, Devon. Are *you* ready? I think from the beginning you've known how I felt. You might be coming around, but can you go through the act?"

Sarah watched Devon stiffen. "What's going to happen? I don't understand."

Gavin turned to her and tried to smile tenderly. "Don't worry about anything," he said, caressing his palm down her cheek. Her nipples instantly tightened at his contact. Shit, he was trying to be caring, and her body was screaming for sex. Sarah shifted as he went on.

"The mark won't hurt you. The way we'll have to place it on though poses a problem. You see, for it to work, both marks have to be put on within a twenty-four hour period. That's not the problem. It's that we all have to be having sex to place it. And if we want the strongest connection, it really needs to be done together and not separate. I don't know about Devon, but I want the mark as pure as it gets, especially since someone's after you."

Sarah felt heat pour through her body. The headache, the tension, everything melted away and disappeared at the thought of both of them being in her bed. Wetness seeped from her pussy, causing her to continue to shift in the seat. The vibrations of the loud exhaust weren't helping either.

"Look at me," Gavin said, easing her face in his direction.

At his touch, a moan almost passed her lips. The need to feel him, to touch him made her unbuckle her seat belt. She was lost, lost in lust, lost in the pull, and mostly lost to the reality that they were driving down the middle of the small island's main street.

Chapter 14

"Come to me."

The sound of Gavin's voice sounded like the sweetest, most seductive music. Hypnotized, Sarah jerked up her skirt and straddled his lap. She rubbed her pussy against his cock, wanting to kiss him. The fact that his gaze rested on Devon and not her was the only thing that broke the trance.

"Do you see how you react? Devon, seriously, watch the road. Sarah isn't buckled."

She looked toward her tense cowboy and slid back into her seat, buckling up. The fuzziness still clouded her thoughts, and her body vibrated with need. As they turned into the parking lot of the apartment complex, she sighed in relief.

"So, are you ready? Can you handle it?"

Devon got out of the truck without answering and walked to her apartment. "Gavin, he doesn't want to watch me with you, does he?"

"No, but it's not your fault. I think it's more of the alpha in him. He doesn't like to share, and he hates the fact that he has to. To him, you'll always be his. I think him knowing what we do and having to watch it are two separate things. Maybe we can convince him together."

Climbing out of the truck, Sarah held her arms around Gavin's waist while they made their way inside. Devon exited the hallway as they walked through the front door.

"All's clear. Sarah, why don't you go take a shower and relax while I have a talk with, Gavin? Is that all right?"

"Actually, it sounds like a great idea."

Kissing both of them softly on the lips, she gathered everything she needed. A smiled came to her face. The sexy, black lace lingerie would do the trick. At least, she hoped it would.

She turned the water on, giving it a few minutes to warm up before she got in. The moment the warmth pounded against her skin, she let her mind drift to thoughts about Devon. Would he stop them before anything even started, or could she get him to submit to her charms? If he didn't, he'd probably be pissed, but it was something she knew she couldn't prolong.

Quickly washing her body, Sarah got out and began dressing in the sexy lingerie. The black lace slip dress was completely see-through, barely covering the smoothness of her pussy. Pink nipples pushed at the material as her arousal heightened. She really hoped she could convince Devon to join her and Gavin. The thought of having both of them close made the wetness flourish.

Pausing with her hand on the knob, she took a deep breath. She could do this. The mark needed to be in place so they'd all stop going crazy, and Tom would hopefully leave her alone. Plus, she wanted to do this.

So she wouldn't have a chance to change her mind, she flung open the door and walked into the living room. The men's eyes stared at her in awe. Devon's mouth parted while he took in her body. Gavin bit his lip as he watched her stand there.

"I thought I'd make this easier on all of us. Things might be a little rushed, but it *is* something we should just get out of the way. I originally planned to keep you two together until you got along, but it seems like that plan went south pretty fast. If you both will follow me, I'll try to make everything as easy on all of us as possible."

Sarah looked toward Gavin and prayed he would catch on to what she secretly planned. "Devon." She stood, holding out her hand to him. He didn't come. With a pained, conflicted expression, he just continued to stare, taking in her body.

Just when fear and disappointment began to leap into her chest from the endless seconds, he walked forward. With his large frame towering over her, she looked into his face. "I want you to focus on me the whole time. This will be hard, and I'm sorry for that, but please try not to stop things."

Devon ran his fingers through his hair. "I'll try. Gavin." He turned around and looked into Gavin's face. "If for some reason I…can't…"

"You will. Devon, you have to. Think of Sarah. She needs to be protected. Who better to keep her safe than you? I'm strong as hell, but you're stronger. We're all in this together. Don't forget that. It's not about you anymore. It's about all of us. When you start looking at us as your own personal pack, things will get easier for you."

"Let's go." Sarah grabbed Devon by the hand and led him to the bedroom. Blood pumped furiously through her veins while she approached the bed. Not knowing what to expect made things worse. They said it wouldn't hurt, but how did they know? Neither one could speak from experience.

Trembling made the steps Sarah took toward the bed almost impossible. Her confidence plummeted as she stared at her comforter. Could she really do this? Although she felt connected to them now, this was permanent, almost like a marriage, except there was no divorcing a mark.

"Sarah, Sarah, look at me. Calm down before you hyperventilate."

She looked into Gavin's face. He stood before her, Devon directly behind. The nearness of both of their bodies wiped everything away. "I'm better now, just pre-wedding jitters, no big deal. This is, of course, more eternal, so to speak. People get divorced every day, but there is no signing your rights over from this."

Before she could feel any more panic, she crushed her lips against his, cutting off whatever he meant to say. The pressure from his hands wrapped around her waist, pulling her closely into Gavin's body, and she was surprised when he suddenly passed her to Devon.

Locking her arms around his neck, she stared into the depths of his eyes. "Remember what you told me while we were in front of the mirror?"

"Of course." Devon nuzzled her nose, a small smile appearing across his lips. "I'll never forget a single second we share together. And I sure as hell haven't forgotten the words I spoke last night."

"Will you tell me how much you love me again, tonight? I think it will help. I know it might not be as intimate for you with Gavin joining us, but I'm a little nervous myself and your words calm me."

"I'll do whatever I can to help."

The sound of the comforter being pulled down behind them drew her attention. She quickly turned back to Devon and placed her lips against his. He was always so passionate, and this time wasn't any different. In slow strokes, he ran his tongue against hers, sparking cravings in her body she could hardly control. All uneasiness left until peace and the rightness of the situation settled in her heart.

"Gavin, get on the other side. I'll put Sarah between us."

The cool sheets pressed against her skin while he laid her in the middle of the bed. Weight settled on both sides of her, and she couldn't help but notice the way her breathing deepened. The rise and fall of her chest slowed while a need so consuming made her clit pulse. Both men's eyes closed at the same time while they inhaled deeply.

"She smells amazing, doesn't she?" Gavin whispered.

"Absolutely mouth-watering."

Devon's gray eyes opened to reveal a darker shade, almost black. Sarah stared, captivated at the change in him. He lowered himself to her lips, kissing her until she was breathless. The taste of him left her gripping his neck tightly as he loomed over her.

The light brush of fingertips trailed down her arm until Gavin reached her hand and lifted it to his lips, placing kisses along the pads of her fingers. With a soft nibble, she moaned into Devon's mouth.

Currents rushed through her core, and she couldn't help but spread her legs wider. Her pussy needed to be touched, and fast.

While Devon continued to tease her with his tongue, she could feel him pull down the small straps of her lingerie. The lace shifted down her ribs as Gavin's hands helped bring the material down farther. Warmth from two fingers gently pulled at her nipple, making her juices increase. From that moment, she was lost. She wouldn't have been able to turn back even if she wanted to, which she didn't.

* * * *

Devon broke his lips from Sarah's long enough to remove his shirt. Surprisingly enough, the fact that he just witnessed Gavin caressing Sarah's breast didn't affect him the way he thought it would. No anger filled him, only the need to please his soon-to-be mate. Just the thought of making her his forever filled him with a sense of satisfaction. She was beautiful as she lay there, heavy-lidded with passion. He wanted to see her like that for the rest of his life.

Lowering his mouth to her neck, Devon trailed down the soft length, teasing her with his tongue. Sarah's body trembled beneath him, a moan filling the room as he lightly bit the junction between her neck and collarbone. The urge to sink his teeth in deeper taunted him and turned his blood into fire. The length of his cock ached with wanting to be buried inside of her.

"You're doing great, baby. Just lay there and let me and Gavin please your beautiful body." He whispered the words feeling her shiver at his proximity.

The sweet taste of her skin filled his senses while he worked his way slowly down to her breast. Taking her tight nipple into his mouth, he pulled it between his teeth gently. Sarah's fingers laced through his hair pulling him farther into the soft, fullness of the mound.

"Devon, Gavin, please someone touch me. I need…"

Lifting his head, he looked toward Gavin, who was taking off his shirt. For moments that seemed to last an eternity, neither moved, but they held eye contact. This was it, the ultimate test, and Devon knew it. He looked toward Sarah and then back to Gavin.

"Gavin, you go ahead."

He nodded and smiled. "I'd love to."

Instead of Gavin touching her, he settled on the bed, lying between Sarah's thighs. Devon watched while he lowered his mouth to her pussy. The first brush of his tongue against her folds brought Sarah into a semi-sitting position. It was all Devon saw because Sarah's arms wrapped around his neck and pulled him down to kiss her.

The image vanished with her taste, but not before he realized how turned-on the vision made him. Hungrily, he kissed her, taking off his pants at the same time. The awkwardness was over. Something happened between him and Gavin when they locked gazes. A strange feeling of peace and understanding had filled his heart, calming him, and suddenly Devon knew everything was going to be fine.

* * * *

Sarah's essence filled Gavin until he could feel fire behind his eyes. Heat raced through him, demanding he show it attention. While his mind tried to force him to hurry, he fought it and took his time thrusting his tongue inside of her pussy. Fuck, she tasted so good. The sweetness teased him. With as much as he loved her juices, nothing compared with the flavor of her cum.

While he trailed his tongue down her slit, so many emotions poured inside of him. It took extra care not to get carried away. Devon took to this a million times better than he thought possible, but the bond was responsible for that. Something, an understanding, passed through them when Sarah needed attention. The fact that the cowboy gave in and let him tend to her needs not only shocked him, but also sealed the deal.

Flicking his tongue over Sarah's clit, she jumped from the sensitivity. He eased the connection until his tip barely brushed against the nub. She let out a loud moan as her hips began to rock into a faster rhythm. Sliding a finger inside, he pushed deep. Continuing the action, he took off his pants and slowly caressed his cock while he thought about different ways he wanted to fuck Sarah.

Mere moments passed, and then tightening drew Gavin from his thoughts. Looking up from between her thighs, Devon sucked on her breasts, his breath coming out in pants. Unfortunately, this first time needed to go fast. There was always time to go again, but what they needed to do was crucial.

Easing another finger into Sarah's tightness, he felt her buck and scream through the spasms. As her scent filled the room, both men looked at each other. He didn't wait. Gavin moved up on the bed.

"Devon, you make love to her first. Sit up and let Sarah straddle your waist. When you're about to mark her, let me know. I'll be behind, waiting for you to tell me when."

Easily, Devon picked her up and placed Sarah on his lap. Slowly, she eased down the length of his cock, moaning as he filled her completely. Gavin grabbed his own length and began stroking it again while he moved in, inches away from her smooth skin. Surprising him, she leaned back against his chest and stared up at him.

"Kiss me, Gavin. Let me taste you."

Hypnotized by her beauty, he complied, lost the moment his tongue swept against hers. A feeling of completion swept through him as they all connected. This was the way things were meant to be. He knew it deep down in his soul. Moans poured from all of them, and like nature taking its course, he knew it was time.

* * * *

Sarah clutched the sides of Gavin's face as pleasure exploded inside her entire body. She could feel herself jerk from the current that rushed through her at the connection they formed. Something told her the time arrived for them to become one. The feeling was in her bones, in her very being.

Gavin pulled his lips back from her mouth, and quicker than what she could comprehend, a slight pain raced into the back of her shoulder, and right above her breast. The bites coming from both of the men quickly turned from pain into instant ecstasy.

Sarah screamed as her pussy tightened around Devon. A twinge began to run through her limbs while a feeling she couldn't even begin to describe seemed to push against her heart, surrounding it in a warm cocoon. All previous pain, disappointment, and sadness vanished, leaving her feeling like a completely different person.

Devon's lips separated with a groan while he began to thrust into her repeatedly. The warmth of Gavin's tongue ran across her shoulder as he pulled her back against his chest. Looking up, she connected with the greenest eyes she'd ever seen. They were so bright they almost seemed to be illuminating even in the light.

She pulled his lips to hers, needing to taste him, all of him. Letting his flavor fill her mouth, she suddenly needed more. Her orgasm was so close, but it eluded her, and she knew exactly what she needed to make her lose all control.

"Gavin, let me lie back," she whispered against his lips. "I want your cock in my mouth."

Easing her to the sheets, he scooted back until she looked up to his thickness. With the tip of her tongue, Sarah traced the length of him. Devon's cock pushed deeper, making her moan. She glanced down and noticed how Devon watched what she was doing. The fact that he seemed to enjoy what he was seeing made her continue eagerly.

Wrapping her hand around the width, she eased the tip into her mouth, tasting the pre-cum that slid across her tongue. Gavin's fingers gripped tight to the sheet next to the side of her face while she took in more of his length.

"Fuck, Sarah. That feels so good. Tonight, I'm going to make love to you real good, baby. You'll see. Devon and I will never let you go without pleasure. Just the thought of my tongue sliding into your pussy is bringing me close."

Gavin pulled gently at her nipple. The words he spoke tightened her insides. Urgency forced Sarah to take his cock deeper inside her mouth. She applied suction with her lips to taste more of him, to have him share his distinct flavor with her.

A load groan echoed off the walls, and greedily, she stroked his length faster with her hand. No longer could she hold off the building orgasm. Devon thrust hard as he swelled inside of her. The effect made her orgasm burst from her body. Feeling the warmth fill her, Sarah heard the sheet tear while Gavin tried to break away from her mouth, but she wouldn't let him.

"Sarah, please. I can't hold off any longer."

"So, don't," she whispered, sliding him back inside.

Warmth coated her mouth. At his essence sweeping through her senses, she heard herself moan. He tasted better than anything she'd ever consumed. She hungrily held onto his thighs until she felt sure she'd savored every last drop.

Devon's body dropped back toward the pillows, while Gavin fell to the bed. Heaviness settled over her, and before she could go over everything they all just went through, she sank into the darkness.

Chapter 15

Sarah awoke to the sound of banging. Groggily, she reached for her pillow trying to bury herself underneath, but as her hand felt around blindly for the feather fluffiness, it was nowhere within reach. Her fingers came in contact with a leg, and she suddenly recalled the events like a tidal wave.

Bolting to a sitting position, she took in the two nude bodies sprawled out on the bed. Gavin was practically hanging off the end of one side while Devon was more curled around the top.

Smiling, Sarah eased from the bed and grabbed her robe. Gavin sat up slowly and another round of banging brought both of them to full consciousness. The clock read nine, but the light still poured through the windows. Confused, she took her watch from the bedside table and checked the time. Devon threw on some clothes and headed out of the room.

"It can't be the next morning. We *all* couldn't have slept that long, right?"

Gavin rubbed his eyes, looking around just as perplexed. "I don't know. I wouldn't think so, but what happened was pretty amazing. I don't even remember going to sleep."

Voices caught Sarah's attention, and she walked to the door, listening closely. The sound of Evelyn's laughter instantly made her smile. "Well, I guess we did sleep all day and night, Evelyn and, I'm sure, Brandon and Stephen are here. I'm jumping in the shower real quick. You can join me if you want. I mean, we don't have to do anything. I just like being with you."

He smiled brightly. "Okay, let me go tell Devon and the others we'll be out shortly."

Gavin brushed his lips against hers and was gone before she could even open her eyes. Sarah walked and turned on the shower, testing the water until it felt warm enough to get in. She had just rinsed the soap off her body when he pulled back the curtain and stepped in.

"Devon told us not to be long. Evelyn's not feeling too well, and they want her in bed, resting."

"Is she sick? She sounded fine when I heard her earlier."

Gavin shifted on his feet and shrugged, stepping in the water next to her. Confused, Sarah waited patiently while he washed his body. Her friend hadn't seemed sick. Evelyn sounded fine. She was laughing.

Stepping back into the water, she quickly got her hair wet. Gavin surprised her by filling his palm with shampoo and working it into a lather. Just the feeling of him touching her, easing his fingers into her hair made heat quickly cover her skin. She suddenly realized his powerful, defined body so close to hers.

A laugh caught Sarah off guard, making her jump. "Now, now, my dear, sweet lover. If you start with those types of thoughts, we'll never make it out of this bathroom, and we have people waiting."

"I'm sorry. You just look so irresistible." Sarah licked the drop of water off his chest. "I think I like you taking a shower with me."

Gavin shuddered beneath her. "Oh, I like it, too, baby, but right now we need to get back to the people who are waiting on us. I promise to make this up to you real good when everyone's gone."

"I'll hold you to that.".

Trying to shake herself from the spell she was under, Sarah rinsed her hair and got out of the shower as fast as she could. He was right. Evelyn wasn't feeling well, and she needed to find out if her friend needed anything.

As Sarah walked into her bedroom, Devon was waiting. The smile transforming his face made her blush. The last twenty-four hours seemed surreal the more she thought of it. She'd never imagined herself this happy again, especially with her ex.

"Everyone's waiting in the living room, but Brandon thinks it will be better to unlock the memories here on the bed. He seems to believe you'll be in need of some…attention, after he's done. We've all agreed that it's probably best for Gavin to take care of you. I'm sure there's going to be a lot to discuss once we know something."

Sarah froze. "Hold on, I don't understand. If Brandon's a vampire, how is he out during the day? Shouldn't he be dust right now?"

Devon and Gavin both laughed. Devon opened his mouth to explain. "Honey, that's just myth. Well, kind of. You see, vampires are sensitive to sunlight if exposed over a certain length of time. They get really bad sunburns if they're in it too long, but I think they're main problem is light in general. It's horrible for their eyes. I think that's probably why they wear shades a lot, even in the dark.

"The older the vampire, the more problems they face. I guess that's where the myths came from. After a certain point, the pain makes it impossible for them to come out during the day, not to mention their skin burns a lot easier with age."

"Oh." Sarah took a deep breath, trying to process everything. As her mind drifted her to best friend, she pushed the fascinating thoughts about what Brandon was away. "I want to speak with Evelyn before we do this. I was told she felt sick."

Devon's smile melted off his face. "Yes, she wasn't feeling very well, but I think she's better now. You and Gavin get dressed, and then I'll send her in."

Sarah watched him walk out of the room. Biting her lip, she couldn't shake the unexplained nervousness. As quickly as she could, she threw on clothes, hardly noticing Gavin getting dressed behind her. Advancing toward the door, she was surprised when it opened and everyone walked in.

"Ev, what's going on? Why are you here if you're not feeling well?"

The smile that appeared across her best friend's face momentarily confused her. Evelyn didn't look sick. The paleness of her skin looked normal.

"Sarah." Slowly advancing toward her, Evelyn turned to look at Stephen and Brandon, and then faced her. "I wanted to wait to say something, but the secret is driving me crazy. I have to tell someone, and I want it to be you, but you can't tell the girls yet."

"Of course, tell me."

The smile slowly left her pale face only to return moments later. "I'm pregnant. We're going to have a baby. Isn't that great?"

Sarah could feel her lips part as she fought to think of words to say. Truly, she felt happy for her friend, but she wasn't expecting the news. She froze in shock. She quickly fought the images of her own pregnancy so many years ago and thought of Ev. Closing her mouth, she walked forward, embracing Evelyn's small frame.

"That's wonderful news. I'm so happy for you. How are you feeling?"

Air brushed against Sarah's neck as Evelyn laughed. "Tired, nauseous. But I couldn't be happier. What about you? I was told you're finally marked."

Heat filled her cheeks at Evelyn knowing, but it wasn't as if her friend hadn't undergone the same thing. Pulling back, Sarah walked to sit on the edge of the bed. "I feel great, wonderful, actually. But come sit by me and tell me more about you. How far along are you? Have you thought of any names, a gender you're leaning toward?"

"I'm not sure yet." For moments, her friend studied her face. "Sarah, please. I know this must be hard for you." Evelyn sat down on the bed, grabbing her friend's hand. "There's plenty of time to talk about the baby. Right now, let's just focus on you. Brandon thinks he can find out more about Tom by doing this. I couldn't agree more. There's nothing to be afraid of, I promise."

Cautiously, Sarah looked up at Devon, then Gavin. "I trust you, Ev. I know you wouldn't let anything happen to me. But really, I'm okay about your pregnancy. Please don't keep anything from me because you might think it will upset me. I'm better now, I promise.

"Let's get this out of the way. I want to hear about the baby. If this is the only way to get you to tell me the details then what do I need to do to get started?"

"That's my girl." Evelyn waved Brandon in their direction. "I want you to lie back on the bed. You need to get in the middle though. Gavin will be on one side of you, Brandon on the other. He's going to...bite you, and then after he's finished we'll leave you and your mate alone while we discuss what we've learned with Devon."

Sarah nodded and crawled to the middle of the bed. She could feel her heart hammering away at what was about to happen. Everyone kept saying it wouldn't hurt. What if it did? What if something went terribly wrong?

Brandon and Gavin settled themselves beside her. Panicked, Sarah bolted into a sitting position. "Devon..."

Devon quickly reached her side. "What is it? Sarah, if you don't want to do this, all you have to do is say so. We'll stop right now."

"No, I just...Just tell me everything will be okay. When you go discuss this, you won't be gone long, right?"

A smile stretched across his face flashing straight, white teeth. "No, I'll hurry back as fast as I can."

"All right." Sarah lay back against the bed and closed her eyes. "Brandon, if you hurt me, so help me God..."

A loud laugh echoed through the room. "No worries. I won't hurt you. Evelyn would have my hide. Trust me, the last thing I want to do is upset her right now her. That woman has a temper like you wouldn't believe. The hormones, my God! "

"I can hear you," Ev said, laughing.

"Right. Okay, Sarah I want you to relax. Gavin, do me a favor and face her toward you and kiss her. She needs to be...well, completely relaxed, if you know what I mean."

Sarah felt Gavin's arms go around her as he pulled her to face him. She looked deep into his eyes, and like every time she rested close to his body, she instantly calmed. The brush of his lips was soft against hers, gently coaxing her mouth open to receive his tongue.

The remaining people in the room vanished with the first intoxicating burst of his flavor. Heat flowed freely throughout her body, increasing the moment Gavin's hand trailed over her hip and up her ribs. When his hand slid against the bed and wrapped around her neck, Sarah was so lost in their kiss, she hardly noticed how exposed her neck became.

Fingers weaved into her hair, at the nape of her neck, pulling her deeper into the passion she felt surging through her. A slight sting pierced her neck, instantly vanishing. A feeling only Sarah could describe as body euphoria filled ever crevice of her being. What felt like instant and multiple orgasms combined made her dig her nails into the muscle underneath Gavin's T-shirt.

His hand tightened in her hair while they moaned into each other's mouths simultaneously. Thoughts vanished into a jumble of complicated twists while Brandon sifted through the events of her past. She knew what he was doing, but her brain couldn't focus, no matter how hard she tried. Overpowering pleasure seemed to be the only thing Sarah could process.

Gripping Gavin's back tighter, she forced herself not to go any further with him, no matter how much she wanted to. As long as she didn't forget people watched in the distance, she couldn't touch him the way she wanted.

"Brandon," Gavin pleaded, breaking his mouth away from hers only for a moment. She knew he wanted her just as much as she wanted him. The hardness of his cock pushed against her stomach, causing her to fight against throwing her leg over his hip to have him closer.

Images began to flash in Sarah's mind, leaving her frozen. Everything disappeared as Tom's fangs sank into her neck. The same pleasure she experienced now made her plead out to him. She couldn't believe the way she could see herself acting. It was so unlike the way she responded to her bets. Promises poured out of her mouth. Promises she knew she'd never keep if she were in her right mind. She could feel the fangs ease out of her neck, and the light blue eyes blazed down at her.

"You belong to me now, Sarah. Tell me you belong to me."

"No," she could hear herself whisper. *"I can't. I'll do anything tonight, tomorrow night, a month from now, but I don't belong to anyone."*

"Maybe not now, my dear, but you'll eventually beg me to make you mine. You promise me a continual affair, something your mind tells me you never do, but I want more than that."

"I said I can't." Sarah could feel the bliss begin to wear off and her mind clearing. *"I said affair. You'd be smart to take me up on my proposition. It's one I've never offered to anyone."*

The length of Tom's cock eased inside of her. Holding in a moan, Sarah focused on not giving into what he wanted. She couldn't belong to him. Her heart would always belong to someone else.

"You will be mine, Sarah."

She wrapped her legs around his waist, ignoring his words. All she wanted to focus on was the way his cock felt sliding inside of her. And those fangs, she wanted to feel them again and again. But she wasn't willing to give herself over to him eternally for it. She knew what he meant, what he wanted.

While Tom thrust into her repeatedly, Sarah could feel herself tightening. The instant her orgasm rocked her body fangs sank deep into her neck again causing her to scream at the intensity of her release. Blackness took over, as she hovered on the brink of unconsciousness.

"When I call tomorrow you're going to be begging me to come get you, to fuck you like I just did. Would you like to bet on it, my dear Sarah? You like bets so much. Don't think I couldn't hear you and

Red discussing me. How about we place a wager? If you meet me, I win. Therefore, you will forever belong to me. If you don't, you of course win, and well…let's face it. You'll belong to me regardless.

"If I wasn't being watched so closely by Channing, I'd turn you tonight. But, he'll know. He knows everything. I can't afford for him to find out my plans. You see, I don't have that many chances left. One more mistake, and I'm history. Masters really don't like their children to make trouble."

Fangs sinking back into her neck was the last thing she felt. Sarah's memory ended, leaving her feeling nauseous. Blinking, she tried to bring the room into focus. Gavin's blurry face looked at her quizzically.

"Brandon, stop," Sarah whispered.

"She's going to be sick. Stop," Gavin snapped.

The fangs exited her neck leaving her feeling weak. The room began to spin, but she fought the queasiness. She wasn't sure what she expected, but it wasn't that.

"How did you fight the pleasure? You shouldn't have been able to resist the lust no matter what you saw. Actually, you shouldn't have cared what you saw. The visions should've gone to the back burner, so to speak." Brandon got off the bed and walked around to face her. Gavin brushed the hair back from her face while she tried to stop the rolling in her stomach.

"I don't know. The pleasure vanished the moment the images appeared. Who's Channing, Brandon?"

"Channing? You can't be serious." Devon walked over to them, anger filling his face. "Channing has been a pain in *my* ass for the last fifteen years. I've only run into him a few times, but every time, there's always some kind of trouble following him around."

"Devon's right," Brandon sighed. "If Channing is Tom's master, then we've got trouble indeed. I don't know him well. My master warned me a long time ago to steer clear of him. He's known in the vampire community for playing dirty. I guess we've found the reason why your stalker has waited a year. Anyone would be stupid to go up against Channing."

"But Tom's afraid of him. Can't we go tell him about what's going on?" Sarah sat up in the bed, swaying slightly. She couldn't help but wonder how much blood Brandon took while unlocking her memories.

"You can't just go up to Channing MacGregor and strike up a conversation. It just isn't done. Plus, we'd never get past his guards, although if truth be told, he doesn't need them. His powers are like nothing you can imagine."

"Powers? What do you mean?"

Sarah stared at Brandon, confused, but he didn't continue. Throbbing began to manifest at the back of her head, and it took everything she had to remain sitting.

"Sarah, I think you need rest. You're really not feeling well." Gavin's soothing voice had her leaning toward him.

"Yeah, that's because she fought the glamour." Brandon said softly. "If she wasn't marked, she wouldn't have stood a chance at fighting it. It's just a headache. The pain should subside soon. I need to make some calls and Evelyn needs rest. If Tom is stupid enough to come over here, then he deserves what you two do to him, but do not leave Sarah. If you do, you'll regret it. He's watching at all times. I guarantee it."

Brandon took Evelyn's arm and led her to the bedroom door. "Oh, and there's one thing I know that Sarah couldn't, and that's his determination to have her. When a vampire locks a human's mind, they leave an imprint. His allowed me to see what he thought at the exact time this took place. She knocked him down a peg by not begging him to stay like every other girl does. He's used to them pleading him to either change them over or be with them forever. That's why he wants her. He knows she won't submit to either."

"We won't leave her," Devon said, sitting on the other side of the bed.

Nothing had turned out the way Sarah expected it to. Besides Channing's name, they didn't know anything new. Now, not only was her head pounding away, her stomach still felt heavy with nausea and the effects of Gavin's kiss. The combination wasn't something she liked very much. At least she knew an aspirin would take care of the headache. As for her craving, well, she'd take care of that as soon as the opportunity presented itself.

"Ev, go get some rest. I'll call you later. And, I want details of everything you've thought of so far, names, ideas for a nursery, everything."

Her friend laughed and leaned her head on Brandon's chest. "I'd be happy to go over everything with you later. Right now, I'm going to nap. It seems lately I can't get enough rest."

"No joke. She's been sleeping all the time. I've never known anyone to not hear an alarm clock in the morning, take a nap during the day, and still want to go to bed early. She sleeps more than a newborn," Stephen said, teasing her. "Anyway, we'll see you all tonight, right? It's movie night at Ayden's. He called me just before we got here. Nicole is anxious to meet Sarah."

"We'll be there," Devon said.

Everyone said their goodbyes, and Gavin quickly locked the front door behind them and brought Sarah medicine. Thoughts of movie night set her heart racing and her head throbbing harder. Finally, she'd really get to meet Nicole. Evelyn spoke of her so frequently, she felt like she already knew her. Sure, they'd spoken on the phone, and been introduced before, but it wasn't the same.

Evelyn and Nicole were a part of something so big, a culture humans never even really thought about—vampires and werewolves. Would the gathering be just like any other, just movies and a group of people hanging out, or would she be walking into something unexpected? Maybe movie night wasn't really a movie night at all. What if the words were code for something else entirely?

"What are you thinking about?" Devon asked.

Sarah jumped. "Oh, it's nothing."

"No, it is something. You looked somewhere else entirely. Are you sure you're feeling all right?"

"I'm fine, I promise. But about this movie night. It is a movie night, right? I mean is that a code word for something else?"

Devon laughed and looked at Gavin, who took Sarah's glass of water and sat it on the bedside table.

"It's definitely code," Gavin said seriously.

Devon's eyes shot to the floor and then looked back up. "Yeah, we should have told you sooner. What we wolves call movie night is really hunting/orgy night."

Sarah looked at Devon and then Gavin, and then back at Devon. "No! You said hunt. What are you hunting? And wait…orgy. I can't see that happening. I mean…I'm not so sure I'd be comfortable with that. I don't know these people and…"

The guys burst out laughing. "Sarah, honey, no one is going to be hunting or participating in an orgy. We were just messing with you. It's movies, that's all. Don't worry. We'd never stay anywhere you would feel uncomfortable."

Heat moved to Sarah's cheeks. She should have known. Devon always did this to her. Why hadn't she remembered the playful side of him? "I knew that," she said, hitting both of them with her pillow.

"Oh, did you now? You should have seen your face." Devon laughed.

"Do I need to smack you with my pillow again Devon Lewis or are you going to quit teasing me? How am I supposed to know what werewolves or vampires do? Besides, you haven't been to one of these movie nights. How do you know that's what they really are?"

"She has a point," Gavin said, his smile slowly falling.

"If it would have been anything besides what Stephen said, he would have mentioned it. We're watching movies and nothing else. You both act like we're walking into an ambush of some sort from our own leader."

No one said anything as they all stared at each other. Why did Sarah feel that's exactly what they were doing? The thought was beyond ridiculous. Evelyn would never let anything happen to her, but the twisting of her stomach didn't calm her suspicions that something was going to happen tonight.

Chapter 16

The two-story, red brick home sat nestled in an upscale Corpus Christi neighborhood, in a subdivision anyone would dream of living in. Dark green shutters trimmed every window facing the cul-de-sac. Hedges lined the walkway that reached a large oak door. The door alone looked impenetrable. It certainly didn't come with the house when Ayden and Nicole bought it. Being a real estate agent, she knew that for a fact.

"Calm down, Sarah. I can hear your heart from here." Devon pulled her body against his while he held her close. "I promise Gavin and I won't let anything happen to you. We're here for movies, nothing else. Whenever you're ready to leave, just signal. I'll think of something."

"Thank you," she whispered. "I don't know what it is. Evelyn would never let anything happen, but I can't shake this feeling like we're all in for a surprise."

Gavin cleared his throat. "Either I'm picking up what Sarah is feeling or I can feel it myself, but I think she's right. Something doesn't seem right."

Sarah and Devon both turned toward Gavin, who was sitting in the passenger seat of the truck. He pulled at the collar of his dark green T-shirt as if he couldn't breathe. His nervousness made Devon tense against her side.

"You stay with Sarah," Devon said, looking around. "I'm going to check it out. When I wave, you can get her out of the truck and bring her inside. If I go in without waving, get her out of here as fast as you can."

Sarah clung to Devon's black shirt, stopping him from opening the door. "No, we're all just a little freaked out over nothing. Let's all go. Really, think about this. Stephen would never set us up. I know him. He wouldn't do something like that. Tom is just messing with all of our heads. The thought of him has us all on edge."

"I don't know. Are you sure you don't want me to check it out first? If it'll make you feel better, I will."

"No, Devon. Let's just go."

The men opened the doors to the truck, and Sarah followed Devon out of the driver's side. They walked around the front, and Gavin quickly fell in step beside them. She didn't hesitate to take their hands in hers. As they neared the front door, Evelyn opened it, standing next to a girl who could easily pass as her sister, if not her twin. Nicole.

"I'm so glad you all made it," Evelyn said, rushing forward and taking her from Devon and Gavin. The uneasiness slipped away while Ev and Nicole led her into a large living area filled with people.

"I'd like to introduce you all to our newest threesome," Nicole said, gesturing toward them. "This is Sarah, Devon, and Gavin. Some of you already know them, some don't. Sarah, these are my mates, Ayden and Trevor. You know Evelyn's, and the three guys on the couch are Jeff, Preston, and Riley. The two guys leaning against the wall are brothers, Nicolas and Nathaniel. And there are three in the kitchen making drinks, Julian, Aston, and Travis. They're all pack and practically live here off and on."

"It's nice to meet all of you," Sarah managed to get out. The uneasiness still existed just along the edge of her nerves. There were way too many people here. The house might have been large, but still, too many strangers set her on edge, and she could tell she wasn't the only one.

The three guys got off the couch, and Ayden motioned for them to sit. Sarah's heart escalated, but she complied and followed Gavin and Devon to the couch to face Ayden and Trevor who sat directly in front of them. Sarah could tell from their expression there was something Ayden wanted to tell them, and it didn't look good.

"Before the movie starts, there's something we need to discuss. And don't blame Stephen, he didn't know. I neglected to mention my guest this morning. Channing!" Ayden called.

Sarah watched spellbound as a tall man began walking down the stairs. There was no denying his beauty, but a sense of power emanated from him that left her speechless and in complete awe. She couldn't feel fear or nervousness. She couldn't feel anything past a need to figure out the mystery that surrounded him. Black hair stood out against his extremely light blue eyes. Tom's eyes.

"Channing, we've discussed this. No glamours on the guests. Leave Sarah alone, or I quit being nice."

Ayden's voice broke the spell, and she shook her head, trying to clear it. She looked back at the vampire and didn't feel anything besides aggravation for what he'd just done. Why was he wearing a business suit anyway?

"You pull that shit again, and I'll rip your throat out," Devon snapped, bolting up from the couch.

"My apologies. I forget myself around beautiful women. And your woman is stunning. Her face reminds me of an angel, flawless."

"Save the pick-up lines. I have a bone to pick with you," Sarah said, standing.

"A beautiful face *and* a lively spirit. You men are fortunate, indeed. I love women with spunk." Channing walked closer to the couch until he stood a mere foot away from Devon. From the closeness, Sarah could feel his power. If she didn't know vampires existed, she'd have pegged him as unstable and steered clear of him. The aura he gave off screamed "run for your life."

"Listen, Mr.—"

"Just call me Channing. No need for formality."

"Fine, Channing." Sarah took a step closer to Devon, bringing her closer to the vampire. She could feel Gavin almost molded against her back. "I…" Gavin cleared his throat, making her turn to look at him. "Sorry, *we*, have a problem with one of your…people."

"My people? You mean one whom I created. Is this correct?"

"Yes," Sarah whispered. "His name is Tom. He won't leave me alone. I've made it abundantly clear over the telephone that I'm not interested, yet he's destroyed my car and he calls nonstop only to remain silent. He's broken down my door! Can you please get him to leave me alone?"

Channing was quiet for so long Sarah could feel herself tense while she waited for him to say something. The longer she waited, the more nervous she became. The fear caused her to look around and see if she was the only one. Evelyn was sandwiched between Stephen and Brandon, Even Nicole was positioned between Ayden and Trevor. Not a single soul in the room was sitting. Everyone seemed on alert, which caused her muscles to stiffen even more.

"Tom has…how do I say it? He's slipped under my radar. I haven't been able to get a hold of him now for weeks. Why do you think I'm here? He's blown his last chance and, therefore, is not to be trusted. I see now why he's neglected to keep in touch. You."

"Me?" Sarah took a step back and collided with Gavin, but he held her against his chest firmly. She instantly felt better having him close. "Since that one night, I haven't seen him. I never led him on. He was given an option I never would have offered had I not been under some type of spell, and still, he refused even that."

"Yes, I believe you. Please do not worry about Tom. I'm on my way out to take care of him as we speak. I'm sorry for any inconveniences he's caused you, and your car will be taken care of. My humblest apologies for the trouble you've been going through."

Sarah's breath caught in her throat as Channing lifted her hand to his lips. He felt so cold, nothing like Brandon, or even Tom. He kissed her palm and suddenly vanished. No opened door, no step backward away from her, just gone.

"What in the hell…" Sarah looked around, shocked. Everyone remained quiet as they stared where Channing used to be.

"I got twenty on Channing," Evelyn said, reaching for her purse.

"Oh, no way, Tom's a determined little shit. I have fifty that says Devon and Gavin get to him first."

Sarah's jaw dropped as Brandon reached into his back pocket. They seriously weren't betting on the outcome of her situation. But…if they were, she wasn't about to pass up the opportunity. "One hundred on Channing. Did you see him disappear? Freaking Houdini if you ask me. Plus, I'd like to keep my men safe with me. Let Channing take care of his own mistakes."

"You people are crazy," Devon gasped, collapsing down to the couch. Sarah immediately felt herself pulled on to his lap. "I understand this is your way of dealing with your emotions, betting that is. But, seriously, we still need to be careful. I'm not trusting Channing to take care of Tom."

"Me either," Gavin said, sitting beside them, placing her legs across his waist. "So, what movie are we watching tonight?"

Relief settled throughout the room. Nicole walked to the flat screen TV while Ayden and Trevor sat back on the couch across from them. Chairs were pulled in from the kitchen as men took their seats randomly throughout the room.

Stephen sat down next to Gavin, placing Evelyn in his lap while Brandon sat on the floor in front of them. Sarah noticed Ev's fingers mindlessly running through his dark hair while she gave all her attention to Nicole. The crowded, comfortable environment put Sarah instantly at ease.

"We're not watching *The Notebook* again, are we?" Evelyn groaned, leaning closer to try to see the DVD box in Nicole's hand. "As much as I love that movie, I'm afraid we wore it out."

"Oh no, not tonight. I thought we were in serious need of comedy, so I picked up something today while we were out. It's going to be great."

"Well, what is it? Brandon asked, scooting forward.

"All in good time, my man," Ayden laughed. "You're going to love it. The idea really belongs to me, but don't tell that to Nicole."

"Don't you dare try to take my credit," she said, turning toward them. "You didn't even notice the movie on the shelf until I picked it up."

"But this was the one I told you about the other day."

"Yeah, but you didn't remember that when we were looking for movies, now did you? I saw it and remembered, so I grabbed the damn thing. Point for me, not you. If I wouldn't have found it, we'd have walked away with *My Best Friend's Wedding* like *you* wanted, but no, we're watching *The Hangover* because of...*me*."

Trevor laughed, and nodded, addressing Gavin. "I told you, it's nonstop. But Nicole, she wins every time. I love it. She gets away with things us guys only *wish* we could."

"Hey, watch it," Ayden said threateningly, looking over at Trevor. Sarah caught his wink and the beginnings of a smile. Nicole gave Trevor a frown but turned back to the DVD player.

"This happens all the time," Trevor whispered back to Gavin. "You should see it, it's hilarious. Ayden always thinks he's winning, but Nicole, she doesn't put up with his shit."

"Trevor, if I thought for a minute you were airing our dirty laundry, so help me, you'd be sleeping in the guest room."

He turned to Nicole, his face instantly serious. "Who me? No way. What would make you think that? Gavin over there has no idea what I'm talking about, do you?" Everyone turned toward their direction. Nicole especially interested, with her hand on her hip.

"Seriously, I have no idea what he's talking about," Gavin said lowly.

"Good, he better not be talking behind my back." She turned back around, and Trevor leaned forward.

"Thanks for covering my ass."

Gavin's jaw dropped as he shook his head confused. Sarah knew Trevor was joking. She'd only met him on two occasions, but both times he seemed to be goofing around.

"I heard that," Nicole said, walking back toward the couch. "Gavin, don't listen to him. He's so full of shit sometimes. You couldn't believe the things he's told me that I completely bought into before he admitted to it being a lie."

"What? I'm easing the atmosphere. That seriously freaked me out. The way Channing just disappeared like that, geez. I have money on that guy. If Tom can hide from him, he's got serious skills."

Nicole glared at Trevor. "We're not going to talk about this, are we, Ayden?"

"No we're not, not in front of the ladies, anyway."

Sarah caught Ayden's glare in Trevor's direction. The movie began, and everyone watched, but her mind wouldn't focus on the large screen. Thoughts swirled around her mind, and she couldn't fight the growing anxiety. Would Channing find him? What would happen once he did?

Regardless, she caught herself laughing throughout the movie even though she couldn't completely focus on it. Once the movie ended, she couldn't help but feel a bit of relief. Even though she enjoyed the time she spent with her new friends, she still wanted to go home and be in her own comforting environment, just her, Devon, and Gavin. The thought made her sigh happily.

"Well, well, someone seems to be in a more relaxed mood," Brandon said from the floor. His head rested against the arm of the couch, but his hand sat upon Evelyn's leg. Her limp body was sprawled across Stephen lap.

"I told you she sleeps a lot. She was out within the first thirty minutes."

Sarah looked at him quizzically. "Does everyone here know?"

"Yes, but she doesn't *know* they know. Wolves can tell even before a home pregnancy test can detect it. Trevor, big mouth, told

Nicole, but she promised not to say anything. Evelyn wants to surprise everyone after the ceremony."

"Oh, okay…Really, wolves know that soon?" Sarah couldn't grasp how that was possible.

"Yes, I'm afraid so. I'm sure Devon can explain it to you. We really should be getting Evelyn home. We have a big day tomorrow. She gets to trade her beloved sports car in for an SUV. She wasn't too happy about it at first, but she knows she gets to drive mine if she ever feels the need."

"We should be going, too." Devon lifted her in his arms and placed her on the floor. "Thank you for inviting us. The environment was refreshing, believe me. It reminds me of Waco."

"We're glad to have you all here. I know how hard this must be on you," Ayden said, suddenly getting serious. "Really, I *do* understand. If you ever want to talk, call me."

"I will, thank you." Devon shook his hand while Sarah gave Nicole a hug.

"Thank you for inviting us over. I had a great time."

"Thank you for coming over. You *are* coming to the ceremony, right?"

Sarah looked at her men who nodded. "Yes, I believe we are. Congratulations, by the way. Is it going to be here in Corpus?"

"Thank you." she blushed. "No, we're having it in Sandia We thought the ranch would be the perfect location. The place is huge, and with as many people that are coming, it'll work out great. It was supposed to be this Saturday, but it seems my dress isn't quite ready and we're going to have to delay it for another three weeks. It sucks, but everything has to be perfect."

"Oh, wow, well, I can't wait to go."

"Good." Nicole smiled. "I'll see you then. Call me."

"Definitely. If you need any help or anything let me know."

Sarah waved as the men led her out of the door. Now she knew why Ev liked Nicole so much. The woman was great. She would have fit in perfectly with them if Sarah had known her before her men came around.

The wind blew hard against her face, nearly taking her breath away. Lightning lit up the sky off in the distance, and she shuddered when she realized it rested in the direction of the island. She never liked the rain. Something about the energy in the air always made her nervous.

Climbing into the middle of the seat, she waited as Devon and Gavin got in. They headed down the road, and she remained quiet while the guys went back and forth over what parts of the movie they enjoyed. She couldn't help but notice how their moods improved significantly being around people they could consider friends.

As they neared the island, the sky lit up at the approaching storm. Sprinkles of rain covered the windshield while Sarah stared at the white line of the road, glowing from the headlights. The chatter echoed around her, but she couldn't help getting lost in her thoughts concerning Channing and Tom.

The handsome vampire scared the bejesus out of her. She couldn't even begin to image the power he was capable of. God help anyone who crossed his path. She had a feeling Tom wouldn't be making it very far. He'd definitely messed with the wrong guy. Remembering him disappearing made her shake her head back and forth.

"You're awfully quiet. Are you okay?"

Sarah looked over at Devon and smiled. "Of course. I'm just tired, that's all."

"Come." Gavin motioned, lifting his arm. "Rest your head on me and close your eyes."

Sarah cuddled under his arm while he wrapped it around her. She felt safe, secure, with both of them next to her. Just smelling his distinct fragrance up close, she could feel herself calm and relax. For the first time, she didn't feel plagued by any memories from her past. As she drifted off to sleep, she'd never felt more at peace.

Chapter 17

The three weeks had come faster than Sarah would have ever imagined. One of her men was always with her when she went to work, but that was okay with her. Spending time with them was wonderful. They'd gotten into a routine and pretty much had all moved into her apartment until Devon's house was finished being built. Waking up beside her men was something new she was getting used to, but definitely something she enjoyed.

Sarah pulled herself from her thoughts and watched, charmed as Nicole walked down the white carpet that was placed between the rows of chairs lining the outdoor aisle. The sun was just beginning to set, casting glows of orange and pink all around the trees surrounding the ranch. The whole scene seemed to come from a movie that hadn't been made or one she hadn't seen.

Everything was perfect. The flow of white silk billowed out all around the dark-haired beauty. Curls sat nestled neatly, piled high on her head, a few escaping down her back. The strapless white gown hugged tightly to her curves, showing off her perfect hourglass figure. Sarah couldn't get over how beautiful she looked. She absolutely radiated with happiness.

Ayden and Trevor waited at the end of the aisle, on each side. Sarah had never seen Ayden smile so big. He looked gorgeous in the black Armani suit. The darkness of his eyes seemed to positively glow with excitement while poor Trevor looked so happy he could cry. His suit matched Ayden's, and together, they took her breath away.

Both Gavin and Devon gripped her hands tighter while Nicole approached the minister performing the service. She held in the tears while her new friend faced both of her mates. Evelyn sat in the row in front of them and her sobs made Sarah's harder to hold in.

Looking around at the nearly two hundred pack and friends, she noticed a lot of them were crying. Almost every female held some type of tissue, but some of the men were wiping their eyes, too. While they were getting ready, Devon told her of Nicole's pregnancy. Sarah had been so caught off guard, she fell while trying to put on her pantyhose. Gavin had caught her, but not before her ass hit the floor. Between Evelyn and Nicole, she'd been bombshelled. But Devon informed her of Nicole already being two months ahead of Evelyn's seven weeks, putting her at around fifteen weeks pregnant.

Devon made it clear that she wasn't to tell a soul, not even Evelyn, although Stephen had probably already told her. With Ayden being alpha, her pregnancy had to be kept a secret from those outside the pack. The men weren't chancing any rival coming along and hurting her or the baby.

With all the news of babies, weddings, and pack rules, her head was spinning by the time they pulled into the ranch. She wasn't sure what she expected, but it sure as hell wasn't the large two story house, sitting on land for as far as the eyes could see, plus some.

The minister's voice drew her attention, and she watched as they repeated their vows and slid the rings on each other's finger. Her heart swelled, and she watched as Stephen let Evelyn bury her face in his chest. Her sobs were so hard, her whole body shook. Tears spilled down Sarah's face while she tried to control her emotions. At least Ev could blame hers on hormones.

"Are you okay?"

She looked over at Gavin. His finger came up, brushing a tear off of her cheek. The tenderness in his touch quickly made more fall. How could things have turned out so perfect? She couldn't believe how lucky she'd gotten to have both of her men in her life.

"I'm fine. Weddings just…"

Cheers echoed throughout the large expanse of open space, and Sarah turned just in time to see Ayden sweep Nicole in his arms and dip her down to where she rested a foot from the ground. Her arms clutched to his neck tightly as his lips locked to hers passionately. Sarah burst into tears at the romantic display of their love. It wasn't every day you saw something like that.

"Oh, honey, come here." Devon embraced Sarah tightly while she fell into some type of unexplainable breakdown.

Cheers went up again, and Sarah looked up to see Trevor eying Ayden with a mischievous smile. His arms gathered under Nicole's bottom so fast she squealed as he gently lifted her. A giggle passed her lips as she leaned in and kissed him for what seemed like forever. Ayden burst out laughing, and everyone rushed up to start congratulating them.

Sarah wiped her eyes and looked up. Evelyn stood staring at her, her eyes swollen and red. When they made eye contact, both girls began laughing. They immediately walked away from their men and wrapped their arms around each other.

"So when do I get to come to yours?" Sarah asked jokingly.

"The guys and I were talking about that last night." Evelyn lifted her hand to show off a large diamond. Sarah gasped, bringing Ev's hand closer.

"Oh my God! Ev!"

She hugged her friend tightly while Evelyn tried to quiet her. "Sarah, shh, I don't want to take away from Nicole's big day."

"Oh, no one can hear us. So when are you thinking about having yours?"

"Soon, before I can't fit into a dress."

"I'm so happy for you, Ev."

"I'm happy for you, too, Sarah. You're mates are good, and they're going to take great care of you. Trust me when I tell you this. Don't hold anything back when it comes to loving them. I know you've been hurt, but give them your entire heart because I can tell they're giving you theirs."

"I will," Sarah whispered. Her chest tightened while she thought over Ev's words. She looked at the men staring at her adoringly, and she couldn't comprehend how everything had come together. The pull had saved her. Without Gavin or Devon, she'd probably still be doing Bets, and where would that have gotten her? Fuck, she sure as hell didn't want to think about that.

Evelyn hugged her, and they walked back to the waiting men. The band was already starting to play. The outdoor reception was in full swing. Darkness was settling in, and lights decorating the large tent twinkled beautifully. Sarah sighed happily and thought someday she'd love to have something like this.

* * * *

Devon watched Evelyn lead Sarah away from the reception and toward the house. Something about going to powder their noses, but he still couldn't get a grip on the uneasiness of letting her go anywhere without him. Gavin's hand slapped across his back, and he turned in his direction.

"So, when are we going to tell her? You know she's going to find out soon enough, anyway."

"You haven't told her yet?" Stephen leaned closer to them, drawing Brandon's attention.

"No, I haven't told her she's pregnant yet."

"Whoa, what?" Brandon said, stepping closer.

"Hell, come on, guys. I just found out three days ago myself. I needed time to process everything."

Devon ran his fingers through his hair. He hated not knowing how Sarah was going to react to the news. Would she be happy, scared, angry, or would she be full of regrets. Shit, if it wasn't for Gavin, he'd already have driven himself insane with worry.

"Well, how do you think she's going to take it?"

He looked at Stephen and looked toward his mate walking in the front door. "If I knew, I probably would have already told her."

Gavin gripped his shoulder, and he felt reassured. The sound of music and laughter floated around him, and he couldn't wait to leave. He needed to tell Sarah and do it tonight, as soon as they returned to the comforts of her apartment.

* * * *

Sarah stopped while Evelyn began talking to one of Nicole's friends, Tara. She excused herself, heading to the bathroom Ev pointed out to her. The need to collect her thoughts and find a quiet space drove her to the safety of the blue decorated room.

Shutting the door, she looked at her reflection in the mirror. Blonde waves hung over her shoulders, covering the majority of her pastel blue dress. She'd had no idea what to wear, but the dress was loose, yet still showed her curves. The square neckline brought out the creaminess of her skin, skin that looked paler than usual, she noticed.

The more Sarah took in her reflection, the more confusion she felt. Something was off, and she couldn't figure out if it was with her appearance or her mood. She rested her palms along the sink and bowed her head, breathing in deeply. Just a few more hours and they could go home. She truly was happy for Nicole, but lately she couldn't get her thoughts in order. The need to lock herself in her home and stay protected left her shaken. What she was protecting she wasn't sure.

The sound of the door knob turning had her opening her eyes. At the light blue gaze, her heart dropped. Sarah walked slowly back, not sure what to do. She opened her mouth to scream, but a hand quickly clamped around her mouth.

"Did you miss me? God, I sure did miss you."

Tom inhaled deeply, running his face against her neck. She screamed against his fingers as her adrenaline kicked in. His hand tightened over her mouth while he crushed her body into his.

"Now, none of that. I'm just taking you to your new home. Don't you want to go home with me, Sarah?"

Shaking her head back and forth frantically, she tried fighting him off, but it was like trying to move a brick wall. She didn't know what to do. What was he planning? Did he just expect to walk her out of the front door and take her away? There were way too many people here. He'd never escape.

She felt her body go calm, and his grip loosen. A knock on the door had his hand growing so tight, she could feel her teeth cutting into her lip. The taste of blood on her tongue nearly made her gag.

"Sarah, it's me. Open the door. You've been in there for a few minutes already. Did you fall in?"

"Tell her you're fine and that you'll be out in a minute. If you don't, you'll regret it."

The hand eased from her mouth, and she took a shuddering breath. If she didn't do something now, there was no telling what would happen. Sarah opened her mouth and let out the beginnings of the loudest scream she could create. The hand clamped back over her mouth, and Tom swung open the bathroom door, exposing a stunned Evelyn.

The moment her friend bolted, she'd never felt more relief. Sarah could feel herself being pulled farther into the house. Yells were erupting from the living room area, but the sound drifted away as Tom opened a back door and pulled her through.

"That was really stupid. Do you know that? It's okay though. You'll pay for that when we get home."

Sarah twisted frantically, jerking against his iron grip. She'd never been happier to be wearing stilettos. Bringing her foot up, she lunged back, catching his shin with the spike. He let out a howl and slowed, but still didn't let go of her.

Tom's fingers weaved in the back of her hair, giving a painful tug, but with her adrenaline in full swing, she hardly felt it. "You keep fighting me and I'll make your change a very painful one. It's going to hurt anyway, but I can extend the agony for hours if I want to."

A car came into view along the lining of trees. Fear like she'd never felt before took over every space in her body. She couldn't let him get to that car. If he did, she'd never see her men again. Some part of her knew that.

"Sarah!"

A combination of people and wolves poured out of the house and around the side. Devon and Gavin rushed forward, followed by Stephen, Ayden, Trevor, and people she'd never seen before. Devon's words regarding the pack refreshed in her memory. Pack always stuck together, and to them, Sarah was pack.

"Don't come any closer. She's mine."

Devon raised his hands, easing forward. "Listen to me, Tom. Sarah can't be yours. Do me a favor and really smell her. I know you'll be able to pick up on it if you try hard."

Tom hissed at him. "I already know you both marked her. I don't need to smell her. It might be painful for her, but she can still be changed."

"Not the mark, just please, just smell her. I know you don't want to do this."

The grip around her tightened as Tom leaned into her neck. He kept his face buried against her skin for what felt like forever. As his tongue traced down her ear, she gagged in his arms. The sound of Tom spitting caused her to try to turn to see him, but he held her tighter. What in the hell was he doing?

"Ugh, you ruined her!"

The anger laced in his voice made Sarah's whole body shake. Her gaze connected with Devon's and then Gavin's. She had no idea what was going on, but whatever it was wasn't good. Tom's fingers gripped her hair, snapping her head back. The scream got trapped in her throat as his fangs sank into her neck.

Both Gavin and Devon raced forward, their bodies noticeably shaking. She knew they were about to shift. She could feel it down to her very bones. At that moment, she should have been scared, but she wasn't. She wanted them to change, wanted them to save her from the psycho who held her against her will.

Wolves raced forward from all angles, and suddenly Channing was there, right next to her. Her eyes locked on him, and before she could process what was going on a snap filled her ears, and she was falling. Gavin caught her just in the nick of time. Wolves jumped on Tom's fallen body, and Gavin quickly buried her face in his chest. The realization that the sound had been Tom's neck made stars dance in Sarah's vision.

"Wait, she's still bleeding." Channing came up to them. "Please allow me to make the wounds disappear. It's the least I can do. I am so sorry I didn't stop him before this happened."

"Sarah, baby, tilt your neck to the side and let Channing stop the bleeding. He won't hurt you. I promise."

She nodded at Gavin and did as he said. Channing's tongue was cold as it traced up her neck. The throbbing disappeared on contact. He bowed to both of her men and walked off with only three departing words. "See you around."

Dazed, she could feel herself being pulled inside and laid down on a bed. She couldn't think. Sarah's hand pressed against her stomach to hold in what little food she'd been able to eat earlier. Devon and Gavin surrounded her, along with Evelyn, Nicole, and their men.

"I'm sorry. I don't know how he managed to get on the ranch."Ayden wedged his way to the bed while Devon pressed a wet rag against her head. "I'm sorry, Sarah. Truly, I am."

"Don't be sorry. It's not your fault." She could barely get the words out of her mouth to assure their alpha.

He leaned forward, past Devon, and looked at her strangely before closing his eyes. As Ayden breathed in deeply, his head lowered and he began shaking his head. The pain that raced through his features as he lifted his gaze to hers made Sarah's stomach flip even worse.

"Does she know?" Ayden whispered.

"I planned to tell her tonight," Devon said, shakily.

"Tell me what?" Sarah's heart pounded against her chest. What in the hell was everyone talking about? Tom's words rushed though her mind. He had said something about her being ruined. What did he mean by that?

"God, if something would have happened..." Ayden stood and took a step back. "Do you think we should get her to a hospital, just to make sure everything's okay?"

"If someone doesn't tell me what's going on, I'm going to be pissed." She sat up slowly, removing Gavin's arm.

Silence settled through the room while everyone stared at her. Ayden slowly made them all leave until just he and her men remained. When no one said anything, she started to get off the bed, ready to do battle if they didn't start talking.

"No, Sarah, relax." Devon placed his hands gently on her arms. "Honey, I meant to tell you this tonight, but I guess you better know now."

"You're damn right I want to know now. What is going on? I'm dying? Do I have some terminal illness or something? If Tom already knew about the mark then how in the hell am I ruined? Tell me! I can handle it."

"You're...pregnant, Sarah."

The air left her lungs as her hand flew to her stomach. Every emotion she could think of flooded her at once. What if Channing hadn't arrived or Gavin hadn't made it to her? What if she wouldn't have screamed, warning Evelyn?

Tears traced down her cheeks, for the first time since Tom had barged in on her. "We're going to have a baby?" The words came out barely above a whisper, and she didn't even wait for his answer. The happiness that swelled in her chest caused her to launch herself into Devon's arms.

"You're okay with this?"

The uneasiness in his voice made her look up. "Yes, of course. Are you okay with it? I'm sorry. I should have asked you."

"Yes, of course. I love you, Sarah." His lips crushed against hers, and the door opening broke them apart. She quickly made her way to Gavin.

"How are you with the news?"

"I couldn't be happier. We're all going to have a baby. What could be better than that!" Gavin's large arms encircled her, and Evelyn's squealing in the background caused her to jump. Laughter echoed out around them.

"How about we continue this wedding?" Sarah said, smiling. "I think we're missing the reception, and I believe they're missing one of the grooms." She looked toward Ayden, who smiled back.

"You have one hell of a mate, boys."

"Yes we do," they said at the same time.

When she walked out of the room, Evelyn glued herself to Sarah's hip. "We're so going baby shopping together. We'll have so much fun picking out clothes and nursery themes. Gosh, I'm so excited," she whispered.

Silk flew through the air as Nicole rushed forward. "Are you all right? I'm so sorry."

"I'm fine. I'm the one who should be sorry. I've completely ruined your big day."

"Not even close." Her new friend wrapped her arms around Sarah and pulled her face down, kissing her cheek. Sarah smiled, hugging her back.

"Now, who wants to hear me sing?" Trevor yelled loudly for everyone who stood in the living room. Yells erupted, and Nicole was lifted by Ayden who carried her out of the door and back to the tent. Sarah wrapped her arms around her men, never feeling happier.

"So, I'm thinking a long soak in the tub, with candles, chocolate, and...apple juice?" Gavin kissed her forehead as they sat at a far table.

"That sounds amazing." Sarah laughed and watched the happy couple cut the cake where Trevor proceeded to take the mic and begin to sing. Everyone was floored the moment his voice filled the air. He sung beautifully, like nothing Sarah had ever heard in person.

"How are you feeling? Are you up for a dance?"

Sarah looked at Devon and smiled. "I'd love to."

Devon nodded and led her to the floor. His arms pulled her close as a slow song started. Sarah held onto him tightly as his body molded to hers. The feeling of his hand spanning across her lower back caused heat to rush through her body. All she could see was him as the sounds of the music quieted from the background. Devon and Gavin's love soared through her, touching places she'd never even known existed.

As the song ended, Gavin appeared beside them. Pulling him close, she held on to both of her men. The three of them together couldn't have worked out better.

"Tonight, we celebrate a new start." Devon looked deeply into her face, his eyes holding so much emotion that it took her breath away. Just before his lips touched hers, she realized what he had said.

"No," Sarah whispered against his lips. "A new start would mean things ended between us. My love for you never wavered." She pulled back and looked at her mates. Their attention was solely focused on her.

"I believe everything happens for a reason. Gavin was that reason." Her hand tightened on the back of his suit jacket. "No new starts. Tonight, the three of us celebrate our happily ever after."

THE END

http://jennifersalaiz.com

ABOUT THE AUTHOR

I live in a small Texas town along the Gulf of Mexico. Family is everything to me. My mother always encouraged my reading growing up. Looking back, my earliest memories revolve around my grandmother, who was always glued to a book. Her passion for mystery is probably the reason I'm so comfortable around a police scanner. Hers was on twenty-four hours a day.

When I'm not writing, cooking, or brainstorming new ideas, you'll see me with a book in my hand. Briefly before I started writing, I was devouring a romance novel every day. For some reason, I couldn't get enough. My husband asked me the question that ultimately changed my life forever. "Why don't you try writing a book?"

At first, I laughed. Write a book? Who, me? Never having written a story in my life, I was intimidated. To satisfy my husband and to sate the curiosity that began to fester inside of me, I did. My first story was my husband's favorite. There was something that ultimately bothered me about it, though. I couldn't write a love scene to save my life. Not one that would fit inside of a "romance" book, anyway. It was way too graphic.

After doing research, I came across the erotica genre and knew this is where I belonged. Details are important, and with my books, the more details during their "coupling", the better.

Siren Publishing, Inc.
www.SirenPublishing.com

LaVergne, TN USA
18 October 2010
201218LV00006B/119/P